My Own Miraculous

By Joshilyn Jackson

Someone Else's Love Story

My Own Miraculous

gods in Alabama

Between, Georgia

The Girl Who Stopped Swimming

Backseat Saints

A Grown-Up Kind of Pretty

My
Own
Miraculous

A SHORT STORY

JOSHILYN JACKSON

WILLIAM MORROW IMPULSE

An Imprint of HarperCollinsPublishers

Excerpt from *Someone Else's Love Story* copyright © 2013 by Joshilyn Jackson.

EPub Edition NOVEMBER 2013 ISBN: 9780062300539
Print Edition ISBN: 9780062307323

10 9 8 7 6 5 4 3 2 1

For my own Sam, for my own Maisy Jane

Chapter 1

I was twenty-one years old when I became a mother, though if I wanted to get technical, Natty happened three years and nine months earlier, inventing himself secretly inside me in the summertime when I was seventeen. That was just biology. It didn't instantly remake me as a mother. I didn't even know that he was there.

Not at first, anyway. I was two weeks into my senior year, training for cross-country and fretting about college applications, before I noticed that my period was late, late, late. All at once I started liking grapefruit and hot peppers, and I wept every time I saw this commercial where a lost dog finds his way back home.

It wasn't possible. I knew it wasn't possible, but I missed a second period, and all my bras and waistbands got snug. I couldn't keep down any kind of breakfast.

I remember carrying the pregnancy test from the bathroom back to my room. I walked slow, careful to hold it level like the box said. My mom was working at our candy store downtown, so I had the house to myself. My best friend Walcott waited on my single bed, all his long limbs pulled in close and his spine bent into a worried hunch. I set the stick down in front of him, on the dresser.

It was low, my childhood dresser, with daisy-shaped drawer pulls and faded Barbie scratch-and-sniff stickers stuck all around the rim of the mirror. It was strange to see a pregnancy test lying beside my old silver pig bank. I sat down by Walcott, and we couldn't look away from that stick. I could see a faint pink line already forming in the test window, telling me it was working properly. The results window wasn't showing anything yet. I leaned forward to pull out a tissue and drape it over the stick, solemnly covering its blank face.

Walcott protested, "Shandi!"

I shook my head. "We can't look for four more minutes."

Still, we stared at the tissue, trying to X-ray eye the impossible answer that was happening underneath it. My old stuffed pony, Lobby-La, lay in a squashy pink flop on the foot of the bed. I picked her up and smashed her to my belly in a hug. The minutes ticked by so slowly that each one felt excruciating, and yet all four were gone too fast. They were over before I was ready to know. It was Walcott who stretched out one long, spider-skinny arm and peeled the tissue back.

I saw the pink plus mark, and the first word I thought was, *Surprise!*

I thought it so loud the syllables reverberated around the inside of my skull, bouncing back and forth all through my brain like a whole crowd had shouted it into my ears. I heard that word exactly that way last September, when a bunch of folks I really, really liked yelled it as they popped up like muppets over the breakfast bar, holding a cake ablaze with seventeen candles and brightly wrapped boxes with all kinds of curly ribbon shooting off the tops.

I didn't say, *Surprise!* though. I said, "Shit!"

That word came out almost as loud as *Surprise!* had sounded in my head, clipped short by panic. Walcott echoed me, instantly. We stared from the stick to each other's reflections, back to the stick, back to each other.

He looked so floored and scared and lost, sitting beside me in the mirror. I didn't look any of those things. I looked blank. Blank and unbelieving, while Walcott was leveled all the way down to the ground. I thrust Lobby-La away, standing up so I couldn't see all the true things that I didn't want, happening on his face.

"It's not your problem," I told him in a flat, dismissive voice.

The wad of cells multiplying inside of me was very literally *not* his problem. I loved Walcott, but not like that. I'd never been with him like that.

If I wanted to get technical, I'd never been with anyone like that.

But *It's not your problem,* was the wrong thing to say to Walcott, who stood up, too, fast and mad.

"The hell it's not," he said.

He stepped in close and grabbed my hand, flipping it

up and then pressing the flat part of his thumb to mine. I could feel the narrow ridge of his scar pressed to my skin.

I knew that scar. He'd put it there himself, for me, on his ninth birthday.

"Hell it's not," he repeated. That scar, fishing line thin, reminding me of all the ways we backed each other. Not one of those ways could have caused Natty, true, but we were both our mothers' only children; we'd grown up together, living close on a slice of mountain with no other houses close by. Walcott was family, as dear to me as my little half brothers down in Atlanta. Between us, there wasn't, there had never been, and there would never be, a *Not your problem.*

Standing thumb to thumb with him—all the fear washed off his face, my other hand pressed to my belly—I understood that there really was some baby, real as Walcott, creating himself inside my body. But that didn't make me feel like I was a mother. Not even after Walcott got his momses to take me to their lady-parts doctor for confirmation, or when he told all my family that I was pregnant, or even when my body swole up and I felt Natty shifting and flexing all his new pieces around inside of me. Not even when the pains started, with Natty wrong way 'round. Not even when they cut me open and lifted him out.

When I saw his squashy potato face with all the long eyelashes in a crumple around his screwed-shut eyes, love rose up in me so mighty and willful, it was like a second living creature I had grown inside myself, right alongside him. Natty opened up his mouth and wailed, and I knew he was *my* person. My person I had made myself.

But having him, even loving him so—it didn't make me a mom; I brought Natty home to a pink-walled room with a daisy-chain wallpaper border and white eyelet window treatments. He slept in a bassinet with a patchwork rabbit guarding his feet, and I slept in my narrow bed with Lobby-La draped over mine. In the mornings, I fed him while my own mom slid fried eggs and melon slices onto my plate, feeding me.

I wasn't a mother; I was just a daughter with a son.

I was a daughter with a son for three more years, until I went to the Lumpkin County High School Lady Indians' Spring Blood Drive, and Natty and I crossed paths with Hilde Fleming.

The blood drive was all day Saturday, in the gym. I was supposed to meet Walcott and his girlfriend CeeCee there at two, but I was a little early. I sat in the car, waiting, and Natty wasn't thrilled about it. He hadn't been thrilled about anything, all day. His nap had been short and restless, and he'd woken up with his forehead in a mad rumple and his eyes overbright.

"This is a terrible idea," he said in his weird, precise little voice.

He'd started talking early, at nine months old, hollering, "Keekee, Keekee," whenever Mimmy's little calico came in sight. Lord, he loved that cat, yelling his one word endlessly and reaching for her tail while she melted around corners and ducked under the sofa in alarm. Then Natty would sit back on his bottom, hooting, "Keeeeekeeeee," after her in mournful tones. He soon added hummy-sounding versions of *mom*: *Mimmy* for me and *Mommy* for my mother; it took her months to get him to reverse those. I had to start calling her Mimmy before he would.

He added *cookie*, *uh-oh*, *Ucka* for Walcott, and on and on, new words every day. He was speaking in whole sentences by the time he was eighteen months old. At barely three he had a huge vocabulary and such oddly accurate diction that sometimes I felt I was in the company of a miniature tax attorney with chubby legs.

Now he was saying, "This hot, hot car is very terrible." He struggled to undo his car seat straps, demanding, "Take me to a air-conditioning!" like a tiny Napoleon.

"Let's wait for Walcott."

I didn't want to go in alone; I'd once been a Lady Indian myself. Sure, the kids I'd gone to school with had graduated and moved on, but I could still run into a teacher I had disappointed. I didn't want to see Coach Wallis, or Mr. Bailing, or worst of all, Ms. Petrie, who tracked her eyes after me all sad whenever I ran into her downtown.

It's not like I dropped out to gobble drugs and play Xbox like Denny French, but I had dropped out. Maybe the school would've let a pregnant Lady Indian graduate; I hadn't tested it. I hadn't wanted to walk the halls with my belly getting rounder day by day. I couldn't face everyone either blaming blameless Walcott or speculating that I'd been slutting it up every other weekend at my dad and stepmom's in Atlanta.

I *had* gotten a diploma via a homeschool program, and I'd rocked the SATs, too. I wanted to study design, and I had a kick-ass portfolio that wasn't all virtual. I'd redone real rooms: Mimmy's and Natty's, plus my dad gave me a huge budget to remake my room at his place. All this won me a spot at Georgia State's competitive interior design program. I ought to march into the school with my head high, their poster child for comebacks. But sitting in the lot, I still felt an invisible scarlet D for *dropout* glowing on my breast, right by a P for *pregnant* and a T for *teen*. Some folks, I'm sure, added an S or a W. Lumpkin County was close enough to Atlanta to draw a lot of city visitors, but in its heart, it was still the small-town South.

So I waited, with Natty grumping at me, "I am sweaty into all my hairs!" until Walcott's ancient Subaru pulled into the slot beside me. Just him.

He grinned at me as we both got out, then came around to lift Natty out of the back.

"No CeeCee?" I asked, as we walked across the lot to the gym.

He shook his head, smiling wryly. "She *says* she got held up, the coward. Needles. She's driving out this evening." CeeCee was in my program at GS. She lived in Atlanta, but Walcott was back in Lumpkin County for the summer, working at his momses' bed-and-breakfast. I lived here with Mimmy and Natty all year round, working part time at our candy shop and commuting to the city two or three days a week to take my classes.

"I want down," Natty announced to no one.

"When we get inside, shorty. I don't want you running around the parking lot," Walcott said, and Natty made consternated eyebrows at him. "Is Natty feeling blue?" he asked, looking to me, but he only found my consternated eyebrows, just the same.

Directly inside, a fold-out table was manned by a Red Cross lady and a pair of cheerleaders. Varsity uniforms, so they were probably seniors. The blond one smiled and handed us our paperwork, while the blonder one peered deep into her phone. They had two more weeks until their summer started; two weeks to bounce about in flippy skirts and high ponies, and then they'd graduate and start their college lives and then their real lives, all correctly.

"I want to get down," Natty said again, even more emphatically, his eyes shiny with mad. Walcott swung him to the floor, and he went monster-stomping off around the table, making explosion noises every time one small foot came down.

Along the basketball court's midline, a white and silver medical version of pipe and drape hid the people who were in the process of donating. In front of that, one short section of the bleachers had been rolled out. Half a dozen people sat waiting for their turn: a skinny teenage girl hunched over a notebook, scribbling. A young couple I knew from Mimmy's church. Two old local guys in running shorts, each thumbing through a section of the paper.

Nearest the pipe and drape, a lady in her fifties sat on the bottom bleacher. She didn't look local. She had on resort wear and designer glasses, and her hair looked like my stepmother's. Rich-lady hair, subtly striped a thousand chocolate-caramel colors with no gray. It wasn't unusual to see folks like her in Lumpkin County. The little town near my house and Walcott's momses' bed-and-breakfast was surrounded by rental cabins and vacation homes. Very touristy, but cute, the kind of place where the store names had extra e's tacked on—ours was called the Olde Timey Fudge Shoppe—and there were wine-tasting rooms and antiquing places.

As Natty monster-stomped loudly past the bleachers, only the woman in the front row looked up. She kept on looking, but in that fond, nostalgic way that told me she was a mom herself, one whose kids were old enough for her to miss having littlies.

Walcott and I sat down near her and started filling out our forms. Natty had stomped himself all the way to the pipe and drape. Usually he'd zoom his cars or look at books near my feet, staying inside an invisible perimeter. When he was a toddler, Walcott called him Orbit Baby, because of how he rotated around close to Mimmy or me as he played.

"Stay on this side," I called to him.

He stopped by a second table, manned by two more Red Cross guys and yet another cheerleader.

"Well, hi there," she said to Natty.

He turned around without speaking and started stomping back. He was usually so friendly. Sometimes overly so—last fall, he memorized our phone number, and for weeks he told it to every grocery-store bagger or bank teller who so much as smiled at him.

He sped up, trotting now, back past me and Walcott as we checked all the boxes that promised we hadn't recently gotten a tattoo, or hepatitis, and that we hadn't engaged in sex for money after 1977. As he picked up speed, he started chanting, "Gee! Gee! Gee!" in time with his feet slapping the floor. He ran straight at a big homemade Go, Indians! banner that was hung low at the back of the gym. He smacked his hands flat and loud against the wall, right under the G.

He spun away from the wall and ran stompy footed back toward the pipe and drape, already chanting, "Oh! Oh! Oh!" in time with his feet. As he passed, the skinny teenage girl looked up from her book, her head rising and swiveling in an odd, smooth movement that reminded me of those velociraptors in *Jurassic Park*.

"Turn the volume down, please," I called.

Natty came even with us, then spun again and started running back toward the banner, still hollering, "Oh! Oh! Oh!" even louder.

"Nathan, I'm serious. Volume!"

He didn't so much as glance my way.

Well, he was three now. Mimmy had told me to brace myself, because the Terrible Twos did not exist; three was the real booger. "You were suddenly so awful," Mimmy had warned, "I'm surprised I didn't flat-out eat you."

An empty threat. I'd been a roly-poly baby, and I'd never seen my beauty-queen mother eat anything that wasn't low fat. But perhaps this was the start of my son's Terrible Threes; he tore past me, hollering, "OH! OH! OH!" even louder, then slapping the wall under the O.

"Goodness, he's saying the letters!" the lady said, impressed. She was Southern, but I'd been right to peg her as a tourist. I could hear a lot of low country in her accent.

I nodded, smiling back at her. "He's addicted to this book where the whole alphabet goes tree climbing, one by one."

"Well! You're in for a ride with one that smart. Believe me, I know." She tilted her head to where the scrawny girl sat at the far end of our bench, her spine straight now. Her gaze tracked Natty as he tore back and forth past her, yelling even louder. "EYE! EYE! EYE! . . . INN! INN! INN! . . . DEE! DEE! DEE!" and slapping his hands flat to the wall under each letter in turn.

Now the old local guys were looking, too, peering out from behind their papers.

"Natty!" I said, but his volume stayed at eleven and I could feel my cheeks heating.

"Son of a gun," one old guy called down to us. "That baby knows his alphabet!"

That made the Red Cross people and the cheerleaders look up and watch, too, and then they all turned to me with wondering faces.

I could feel my shoulders retracting, folding inward. This school was the last place on the planet I wanted every eye on me.

Walcott leaned in close. "God, I'm dumb. It must be crappy, huh, coming back to your *Almost Mater*. Why don't you and Natty go get frozen yogurt?" he asked, then added with mock-superiority, "They really only want me, anyway."

He made me smile in spite of myself. "Oh, shut up, Mr. Universal Donor. We can't all be blood sexy. Some of have to settle for being blood cute."

"Aw, don't feel bad," he said, overly earnest. "I'm sure a lot of people really *like* B negative."

I relaxed a little, and they had all stopped looking at me now, anyway. They were too busy marveling over Natty as he ran and yelled the rest of the letters in order, left to right.

"My girl was exactly like that at his age, and her IQ is off the charts," the low-country lady told me, smoothing back the dark wings of her hair. "Hilde's only fifteen, and she's already finished high school. She's going to start at Elon University in the fall."

The teenage girl turned toward us at the sound of her name.

Snow White, I thought, as I took in the dark hair and chalky skin, the only color in her face her cherry-red lip gloss. And then, looking closer, I thought, *Or maybe Snow White's corpse.*

Hilde was skinny to the point of being gaunt, with lavender circles traced deep under luminous, pale eyes. They were arresting eyes, wide set and too big for her face. Her hair hung limp, so black it seemed devoid of color. She turned back to watch Natty without speaking. They all watched.

I hoped he would stop at the end of the banner, but when he got to the punctuation, he yelled, "Escamation point!" once before starting over, yelling the G and running back toward the word *Go.*

Now a middle-aged fellow who had been drained already was peering out from around the curtain, munching his Nutter Butters. A woman in a scrubs top came around, too, wanting to catch the second act of the Natty Knows His Letters show.

He hit the wall under the G, and started yelling the O without bothering to pivot and run away from it first. He walked down the wall, yelling each letter and one-hand slapping the wall under it in turn. I started to get up, but Walcott put a hand on my leg.

"Nathan James Pierce," he called out, deep and boomy. It was his *You're five seconds from a time-out* voice, and Natty finally paused. He turned to look at us, the fold between his eyebrows that I called his grump line visible from here.

"Come sit down!" I told him, sternly, and his whole face set itself into the very shape of mutiny.

He called back, "No, Mommy! I want to run *Go, Indians.*"

I felt the pause, a sudden breathless silence, as all the strangers understood what had happened before I did.

"What did you say?" I asked him, but it came out too soft for him to hear it.

On all the watching faces there was something more than interest, now. It was almost as if he'd scared them. Natty was the only three-year-old child I really knew, but the shocked faces focused on my child told me loud and clear that this was not normal. This wasn't normal at all.

"Did he just read that?" Walcott asked.

I shook my head, because he couldn't have. I looked around, hunting a simple explanation. Was there a picture of an Indian, maybe? The end of the banner only had a feather and a tomahawk, and anyway, what would a picture of "Go" look like?

Only the older mother in her expensive glasses seemed unperturbed. "*Just* like Hilde," she said. "She taught herself to read when she could barely walk."

I glanced at Hilde—hunched over, emaciated, white as a corpse—and I didn't find this comforting. Not remotely.

"He can't read," I said to the older mother.

And immediately, like a refutation, Natty called again, "I want to run *Go, Indians*!" He pointed one emphatic finger at the banner.

I found myself standing, and the paperwork slipped from my hand and landed in a scatter on the floor.

Hilde began scooting toward us, swiveling her feet first, then sliding her butt along the seat, coming down the bench like a sidewinder, but never taking her eyes off Natty. She stopped beside her mother and leaned around to look at me, and those pale, wet, froggy eyes, so big they bulged a little from the sockets, seemed like a metaphor for all the eyes in the world, staring at us in this shame-soaked building, the last place on earth I'd ever wanted to revisit.

"He's special. Isn't he." She spoke flat. Not a question so much as a confirmation of a thing she'd already decided.

Her mother gazed at her with fond indulgence. "Just like you, sugar."

I walked away from them without answering, crossing the gym to Natty. I felt like every step I took was echoing and calling even the eyes of insects and angels to stare at us.

I knelt down and took him by his arms. I looked down into his face. "How did you know that banner said, 'Go, Indians'?"

I was hoping he would say Walcott told him, but Walcott was as gobsmacked as me, as shocked as every staring asshole in the place.

Natty only said, "But I did to want to run *Go, Indians*," in a pitiful whine.

Then I noticed how hot his arms were, how his hair stuck up in sweaty tufts. I put one hand on his forehead, and it was blazing. Touching him, I was surprised my fingers didn't blister.

"Crap," I said, taking hold of his arms again. "Are you sick?"

"No," he said, grumpy, because of course he was.

I started to call for Walcott, but right then Natty's spine stopped working and his knees buckled. He flopped into an instant crumple, and only my grip on his arms kept him from smacking hard onto the floor.

"Natty!" I screamed. "Natty!"

He twitched and rolled in my arms, eyes open but so, so blank. His lips parted, and a froth of white foam dripped out between them.

I didn't think. I couldn't. Mimmy would have known to call for whatever nurse was right behind the pipe and drape—there had to be at least all kinds of med techs—

but that never occurred to me as Natty jerked and trembled and his blank eyes rolled back into his head. I swung him up against my chest. I held him close, and I sprinted for the door, running us away from the closest help, screaming Walcott's name as we went.

Chapter 2

The hospital was less than three miles away, but we had to go right through the heart of downtown to get to it. I don't know how Walcott did it without killing some pedestrians. He drove so fast, horn blaring, not so much as pausing at the stop signs.

I sat in the back, clutching Natty close. I hadn't put him in the car seat. He could choke on the foam that drooled out between his lips, painting his slack cheek. I held him with his face turned sideways, calling his name over and over as he spasmed, and Walcott careened down the road. By the time he screeched to a halt in the turnaround by the emergency room entrance, Natty had stopped seizing, but his eyes were made of glass and he didn't answer me for all my calling. He was breathing, but he was only a little breathing body. There was no person in it.

I spilled out, running through the automatic doors

with Natty bouncing and jouncing bonelessly against me. Walcott left his car where it was and came in right after me.

A calm and smiley nurse manned the registration desk. She took one look at us, at Natty's still, small form, and led me right to the back. She was saying something, her tone very soothing, but the words washed past me, nonsensical and lost. Walcott pulled my purse off of my shoulder and stayed with her to do the paperwork, digging for my insurance card and ID.

A different nurse, tight-lipped, with eyes that looked to me as hard as flint pebbles, pried Natty from my hands and led me to a curtained cubicle. She lay him down on the bed, checking his temperature with an ear-thermometer, while I said, "But you should get a doctor. He should see right now a doctor."

She spared me an irked glance. "You need to calm down. His temp's at one-oh-two, so this is likely a febrile seizure."

I didn't know what a febrile seizure was, and I could not calm myself. Not when this thin-lipped bitch was touching the inert body of my son with such casual hands, business-like and cold. I babbled on, begging her to go and get a doctor, now, telling her about his eyes rolling loose in his head, about the foamy spittle on his lips. Natty lay in a limp string, and she went right on peering in his mouth and up his nose and into his ears with a pen light, telling me I needed to relax, like we were at a spa.

She finally turned to me—turned her back on my terrifyingly still child!—and said, "Ma'am, I need some information. Do you want to help your son? The best way to help your son is to take a deep breath and tell me what I need to know."

She stood between my son and a doctor, this woman made of bricks. I gulped and nodded, moving to the other side of the narrow bed to be by Natty. I looked down at him, petting his floppy little arm, and said, "Ask, then."

Natty stared vacantly off into the corner, as the nurse said, "Febrile seizures are quite common at this age, but to be sure, I need to know if there is any history of epilepsy in the family? Or type one diabetes?"

I glanced up at her, uncomprehending. "I don't have epilepsy. We don't have diabetes. You think Natty has epilepsy?"

She said, cool as a robot, "Ma'am, I told you. I think this is a febrile seizure. We're just ruling things out." Natty lay so very still. "What about on the father's side?"

"He doesn't have a father," I told her, unthinking. Mimmy always handled this kind of question: at the pediatrician, at his preschool, at this very hospital when I gave birth. She'd also smoothed down the town gossips and any friends who had questioned me directly and gotten a sharp *You should mind your own damn business* for their trouble. I'd had no practice answering, and anyway, all I could see was Natty. I bent over him, still petting his arms, his face, as if the sweetness in my hands could call him back to me.

After a pause, the nurse said, "You mean, you aren't sure who the father is?"

She said it in such a judge-y, snotty tone that I actually paused in all my panic and looked up at her, this woman who stood between my kid and a doctor. How much longer would she stand if she thought of me as just another careless teen mom with a throwaway kid? I felt that invisible red letter glowing on my breast again, an S this time for sure, and I snapped the truth, the truth I never said out loud anymore. I snapped it at her without thinking.

"I mean he doesn't have one. I mean I was a virgin until a full year *after* he was born."

She was clearly taken aback, and I felt the very air in the room change as her overcool, professional demeanor dropped way. Her eyebrows got away from her and headed straight north.

Her impatient gaze changed, too, but not to kindness. To a specific kind of carefulness. To a certain understanding.

"Okay," she said, drawing out the second syllable very long. "So, no epilepsy or diabetes that you know of. What about mental illness? Is there any history of mental illness? In the family. That you know of?"

I felt my face flush. I shook my head no, back and forth, but she clearly thought she'd found the slot where I belonged. Not a slut, just a crazy person, with a crazy, seizing son. That's what she thought, this woman who had all the power.

"I didn't mean that like it sounds," I backpedaled. "Can you just tell me what a febrile seizure is? Or maybe get the doctor to come tell me?"

"Sure," she said, way too soothe-y, the way a person

would speak to a feral dog that might be snappish. "How did you mean it, though, exactly?"

Then we stared at each other, me acutely conscious of Natty zoned out beside me, needing some kind of help that I didn't know how to give him, her implacable, but also some gross kind of over-interested.

And then, and then, thank God, I heard the dulcet voice of Mimmy, rising clear and commanding over all of this pure hell. Walcott must have called her; our candy shop was only a mile away. She sounded close, outside and to the left of our curtained cubicle.

"Shandi? I hear you talking, where are you? And why is this child standing here bleeding? Whose bleeding child is this, please?"

"Mimmy!" I called, like a drowning girl, my voice sounding so teary and so high. "Mimmy! Mimmy!"

I heard the click-clack of her heels coming six steps closer, and then she thrust aside the curtains. They moved back with a blessed scraping sound, and there she was. Mimmy. Beautiful and terrible and calm, calm, calm.

"Can someone come and help this bleeding girl?" Mimmy called over one shoulder.

I blinked, disbelieving; the pale teenager from the gym stood beside her. Hilde, her mother had called her. Unmistakable, with her lamplit eyes and dead black hair. She peered into our cubicle with a creepy, close-lipped grin, so serene it took until then for me to notice she had a long carpenter's nail spiked all the way through her left palm, so deep I saw it coming out the other side. Her right hand was cupped under the nail, catching the slow drips of bright red blood that fell from the tip. I gaped at her, and the ends of that smile curled up even higher.

"I heard what you said. But I knew. I knew already," she told me, low, as Mimmy stepped past her into the cubicle.

Mimmy came to the other side of the bed from me, close to the nurse, and bent down to Natty. She put her hand on his chest to feel his breathing and she called his name. When he didn't respond, she said over her shoulder to the nurse, "Exactly what is a febrile seizure?" and I knew Hilde was not the only one who'd been listening long enough to hear me claim my miracle.

"I didn't mean to bring it up again. I only . . ." I said to her, but Mimmy looked up at me with such soft eyes.

"Shhhh, baby, I'm here now," she said. "You don't have to explain." And then, cool and collected, to the nurse, "A febrile seizure is . . . ?"

The cold nurse swallowed and said, in a tight voice, "A simple convulsion caused by a fever. This child has an ear infection, and that's probably what triggered it."

"So it's scary-looking, but not serious?" Mimmy asked, voice imperious, but her eyes still so soft on me, her gentle hand on Natty's chest.

"Not serious at all," the nurse said. "If the brain overheats, it sometimes reboots itself, the same way a computer will. It's very common at his age; he could come around at any second. I'm actually more concerned about your daughter. She seems to—"

At once Mimmy was straightening, turning to the nurse, smiling and stepping in close to take her arm.

Mimmy was so ridiculously pretty, so poised, that all her life people had simply made way for her. So much prettiness draped over a slim spine made of steel—Mimmy bowled everyone right over. Not just men, either: women, babies, dogs. Anything with eyes would stop to gaze at all the ways she was symmetrical, at her skin's sheer glow, at the impossible rich colors of her. While they paused, she stepped into the spaces that she wanted, and then kept them. I was cute enough, with my dad's dark, thick hair and a round, pixie-nosed face, but nothing like her. Now Mimmy turned the nurse away from me, murmuring in honeyed tones, handling this part the way she always had. She turned her beauty and her charm full force onto that cold nurse, dazzling her into compliance.

I was left standing by Natty, with Hilde's gleaming gaze crawling back and forth over both of us. Another drop of blood fell off the nail's point, red as her cherry lip gloss. It spattered onto her pale palm.

"It is the child," Hilde whispered, reverent, to me and only me.

I had no idea what she was talking about, but I answered on pure instinct. "No, it isn't."

"He's come," she intoned.

"No, he hasn't," I said.

Before she could say more, the nicer nurse from the front appeared around the corner. "There you are! Miss Fleming! Your mother is about to have a kitten, and what were you thinking, slipping off while she was in the ladies'?"

Hilde docilely let her body be turned and led away,

but she kept her head swiveled, staring back over her shoulder at my child.

As they left the nicer nurse was saying, "You stay put until we can get you into X-ray. You could injure your hand farther!"

I ran two steps forward and I pulled our curtain shut. Something had gone bad wrong in Hilde's head. Whatever it was, it was worse than the nail in her hand . . . that nail, its perfect placement in the center of her palm, it reminded me of something. I couldn't quite connect it for a moment, and then I had it. That hairline scar down Walcott's thumb, and that nail in her palm, both so exact and centered. I came to a cold understanding then: Like Walcott, Hilde had done it on purpose. Of course she had. But not for a sweet reason. For a crazy, crazy, crazy one.

I should have realized it before. She couldn't have accidentally gotten nail-stabbed at that clean gym. Had she crept under the bleachers, taken the nail from her bag and . . . I tried to imagine the amount of will and mental illness it would take, to drive a nail right through the center of your own hand, hard enough to make the point come out the other side. Then what? Had she told her mother, "Oh, I tripped and landed on a nail?"

Her mother was an idiot if she thought this was an accident, and yet they must have told the nurses that it was. Otherwise they'd be taking Hilde to Psych instead of X-ray. Also, I'd just had a short seminar in exactly what it sounded like when a nurse talked to a crazy person, and Hilde's nurse wasn't talking to her that way. Not at all.

All that talk about *It is the child* plus her do-it-yourself stigmata hand—Hilde was rocking some kind of spooky Jesus complex. And if she carried nails for self-impalement as a matter of course, what else might she have secreted in her big handbag?

I shuddered. I should definitely tell a nurse, although I doubted I had much credibility with mine.

When I turned back around, Natty's eyes were focused on me.

"Hi, Mommy," he said.

I forgot about Hilde Fleming. I forgot everything in the sweet wash of relief that spread all through me, and I burst into tears.

"Hi, Natty," I said around my sobs.

Mimmy and the nurse stopped conferring and the nurse said, "There now, you see?"

Whatever Mimmy had been telling her, it had made her cold eyes on me slightly kinder. Or maybe the nurse had gotten too Mim-rolled to function at full bitch. It happened.

"Hi, baby," Mimmy said to him.

"Why is Mommy crying?" Natty asked her.

"Oh, she's just happy," Mimmy said. "You got a fever, and she was all worried, but now you're okay, and look! We're all so happy!" She smiled up at me, soothing my son and me at the same time, taking care of us, like always. "Mimmy's here now," she crooned, petting Natty's sweaty head, but her words were meant for me as much as him. "Mimmy's going to take her babies home."

Chapter 3

Forty-eight hours after our emergency-room visit, the antibiotics had Natty feeling himself again. He popped up at six A.M., ready for breakfast, pinging off the walls with pent-up energy. The kid needed to run it off. I texted Walcott—he got up early every morning in the summer to write, so I knew that he'd be awake—and we all three drove to a park Natty liked on the town square.

Walcott and I sat side by side on top of a picnic table, our feet on the bench, watching Natty dig trenches in the sandbox about ten feet away. Downtown was dead this early, with only the diner open, but I hoped another sunrise kind of kid might show up for Natty to play with.

"Why don't you go slide," I called to him. Beyond the sandbox, the park had two cute wooden play forts. Kids climbed up a ladder and through a hole in the floor to get in the first one, then crossed to the other through a clear plastic tube. The second one had a slide for an exit.

"No, thank you," Natty called back.

"Keep your head in the game, Pierce," Walcott told me. He'd brought his iPad, and I was trying to help him solve the Rubik's Cube app that had been making him so crazy.

"I could swing you," I called to Natty.

"No, thank you," he yelled.

I said to Walcott, "I hate sandboxes. Cats come and poop in them. You know they do. Why would you put a giant litter box in the middle of a kiddy park?"

Walcott took the iPad back and started messing with the cube himself. I'd managed to get one side to all be yellow, but in just a couple of moves, he thoroughly wrecked it. Walcott was an English major.

"Dammit," he said mildly, and poked it again. Every time he touched it, he made it worse.

"Natty!" I called. "Go slide!"

Natty blew air out his mouth so loudly I heard it from the picnic table, but then he obediently got out of the sandbox and trotted to the first play fort, climbing up into it. We watched him cross through the tube and then come whizzing down the slide. He ran around to do it again, and I looked back to the screen.

"You're terrible at this mathy kind of game," I told him. "Get the new Angry Birds."

He shook his head, sad. "Angry Birds is secretly geometry. Game apps are all math, one way or another."

"So go to Facebook and make CeeCee play Words with Friends! This is torture," I said, but it was addictive torture. Walcott and I both bent over the screen as Natty ran the ladder-tube-slide in an endless, churning circle that boded well for today's nap. I couldn't make more than one color line up, but I could intuit that there was a pattern. I fixed the yellow side, not sure exactly how I was doing it. The other five sides were still a mess. As I spun the cube with my finger, it occurred to me that Natty's last circuit through the play fort had started a couple of minutes ago, and he hadn't yet come down the slide.

I called his name, and waited, head cocked, but he didn't answer. I got a little spine chill.

"He's in the fort," Walcott said.

But the chill didn't pass. "Let me go look."

I called out "Marco?" as I crossed the green. Natty might ignore his name, but when one of us said "Marco," Natty always came back "Polo." Not answering "Polo" was a cheat, Walcott had told him last year, after a fifteen-minute tearing search through all the house, when two-year-old Nat decided to play hide-and-seek and didn't tell us. Natty was such an earnest little person. He would never cheat. If I said "Marco," he came back "Polo," always. But not this time.

"Marco?" I called again.

In the resulting silence, my heart learned the cramping beatless stutter that every mother comes to know, the one that happens when your kid drops out of sight at Dillard's or the Kroger. Nine-hundred-ninety-nine times out of a thousand, he's crawled under a clothes rack to see a neat bug or run ahead to the sugar cereal aisle. But that thousandth time. That thousandth kid. For five seconds, I was so scared I was the thousandth mother, the one who looks away from her child, just for a moment. When she looks back, she sees only dead air, empty and already cold. I was so scared to be her. I broke into a run as I passed the sandbox.

I climbed the ladder, stuck my head and shoulders through the hatch—and there he was. He squatted with his back pressed into a corner, arms hugged around his own knees. Exasperated relief washed through me. He was all I could see: Natty, safe and present, his forehead in an angry rumple and his mouth scrunched into a wad.

Then my eyes adjusted to the dimmer light, and I saw Hilde Fleming was up there with him. Dirt streaked her pale, flat face. Her lips parted as our eyes met, and the tip of her tongue poked thoughtfully out, very pink and pointy. She'd folded herself into the corner opposite, on her knees. She held her white-bandaged hand in close against her chest, like any creature with a wounded paw. In that small, dim space, she was close enough to Natty to be breathing in the air my son had just breathed out.

In her good hand, she held a pair of sewing scissors. The sunlight came through the fort's slatted roof in stripes, lighting up the silver blades. They went in a nasty curve like the beak of a small but wicked bird. In the other hand, she held a lock of hair. It was light brown and straight and very fine, as familiar to me as my own. I looked back at Natty and this time clocked the bristle of cropped hairs sticking up like a chicken tail at the very crown of his head. My whole skin blanched cold.

I came up another step and lurched the top half of my

body toward my kid. He reached for me and I grabbed
him, pulling him across the floor to me. He clipped his
legs around my waist, arms wrapping tight around my
neck. I could feel his small body shaking.

"She cut my hair!" he whispered fiercely, and I realized that he wasn't shaking because he was scared. He
was outraged.

I stood on the ladder with only the top half of my
body poking up through the hatch, holding my kid close,
and I bared my teeth at Hilde Fleming. My breath came
out in a wordless hiss. It was an animal noise, rising up
from the animal feeling that poured through me. I could
have bit her open, in that moment, could have torn her
face to bleeding ribbons with my hands.

The violence rising up inside my middle scared me;
I had never felt this in myself before. I backed down the
ladder, one-handed and very fast.

As soon as we touched ground, I set Natty on his feet.
I knelt down, checking him over. As far as I could see, the
only thing she'd cut with her wicked little scissors was the
sprig of hair. But this was the girl who put a nail through
her own hand. What if I'd been thirty seconds later? An
awful picture came into my head: Hilde going after my
son's pretty eye with those curved blades, short and sharp.
I shuddered, and I couldn't get my heart to slow, not a tick.
I could maybe keep myself from biting her, but I wasn't
done with Hilde Fleming yet. Not by half.

"You're fine, bunny," I said to Natty, and I made my
voice be mild and cheery in spite of all the animal raging
inside me. He blinked up at me, believing it.

"I don't like that girl, though," he told me.

"Me either!" I kept my tone light, as if we were discussing the spoiled kid who tried to boss everybody at his preschool. "I need a sec—run go see Walcott? You can have a turn on the iPad."

He grinned and trotted instantly off toward the table. Last week Walcott had downloaded a preschool app called Dinosaurs!, and Natty was obsessed with it. I watched until I saw Walcott had eyes on him, and then I turned back to the ladder.

My blood galloped through me, red and hot. I'd seen Mimmy like this once, when Nat was barely four months old. She and I had turned to look at a dress displayed in a shop window. When we turned back, an oily-looking man, not a local, was bent over the stroller, hovering so close to the baby. I blinked, only surprised, but Mimmy was already moving, bulling in between them, physically shoving at this fellow who was twice her size. He skipped back, blanching. Her shoulders stayed braced and her neck was so tense that it looked made of cords. He'd apologized and I'd apologized and laughed it off, smoothing things over, but as he walked away, Mimmy stayed bristled up.

"He's not right," she said. "If you see that man again, you take Natty and you go the other way." Staring holes in his retreating back, she had a look on her face that I had never seen before, her upper lip curled back to show her teeth, her eyes slitty and mean. I could feel the same look on my face now.

I hadn't known I had it in me.

I went up the ladder, poking my top half back through the hole, legs braced on the ladder.

Hilde still knelt where I had left her. She'd put the scissors away into her big purse, trading them for the same purple notebook that she'd had at the blood drive. She was writing in it as I reared up over her, my head almost touching the ceiling. I leaned in, putting my face close to her face.

"What the hell is wrong with you?"

She looked back at me, thin bands of sunlight striping her face, and the shine caught in her glossy eyes, yellowing them. Her head tilted slightly to the side, regarding me like I was an odd species of beetle that had come along to interrupt her business. I hadn't ever been so close to her. She gave off a faint electric lemon smell, like ozone gone a little sour.

Instead of answering, she turned her notebook toward me, showing me the page she was working on. It was filled with numbers, symbols, too random to be true math. There were curls of hand-drawn smoke filling every bit of blank space, the paper so overworked it was almost black with ink. She'd cut out tiny bits of magazine pictures, too, collaging them into the bad math, like they were part of the equation: a candle with a human eye glued where the flame should be. A long, legless dog body with a baby's face. A manicured model's hand with a nail drawn in, jutting through the palm.

The numbers and symbols were written in a spiral, like a nautilus shell that had the only patch of clean white paper at the genesis. That patch was blank, but not empty.

Sunlight gleamed there as the few strands of Natty's hair she'd taped into the middle caught the light. "He solves it. Do you see?" Hilde whispered, so intense. "He's the other half of me. You see?"

I saw she needed medication. I saw that she was so, so not okay. I skipped reason and told her straight, "Stay away from my kid."

To my surprise, she nodded, solemn, and said, "We all will. After the miracle."

I blinked. She was so matter-of-fact, for a crazy person. "What miracle?" I asked, but that was the wrong question. "Wait—who is 'we'?"

"I couldn't do it by myself. I've tried and tried. But I found him, and we'll make the miracle happen together," she said, like it was perfectly normal to creep up on a three-year-old in a play fort to make him change his juice box into wine. Then her lips tilted up in a prim, instructive smile and she added, "After we're one, you must call us Emmanuel. The angels sing that it is so. I know you hear them, too." Her voice was high-pitched and bright with conviction. My spine shuddered like a tuning fork that had just been struck. There was an odd compelling power in her stillness and the sheen of her round, wet eyes; last semester I'd had to read *The Crucible*, but until this second, I hadn't understood how the Salem Witch Trials could have happened.

I said, "You keep your crazy bitch scissors away from my kid."

As I spoke, her gaze twitched sideways, like she was looking at my ear tip or just past my shoulder. She said, almost sorrowfully, "You're right. She's not yet fit." She wasn't talking to me. Not at all. "We'll have to help her see." I was breathing hard, but it was like the air near her was dry of oxygen. Then she did speak to me again. "This is our secret, little Mary. You know what he is. I'm just like him."

"He's nothing like you," I spat back in a pure reaction that had no thought behind it.

"Oh, no, we're the same." She leaned in closer to me. "I was born of a virgin, too," she confided, and then added slyly, "My mother and father still don't share a bedroom."

So she'd definitely heard me at the hospital. She'd already decided that Natty was "special," at the gym, and I had inadvertently confirmed it.

I realized then that she hadn't put the nail through herself just because she was a nut bag. She'd had an agenda. She'd watched me run out of the gym with Natty as he seized and shook, and she'd wanted to go to the hospital, because where else would I be taking him? She'd caused her own injury so her mother would take her along. So she could follow us.

No, worse. Follow Natty. God, she must have done it immediately, seconds after Natty seized, to get there so soon after us.

There was nothing I could say to her now that wouldn't make things worse. I slid down the ladder, jumping the last rungs to land on my shaking legs. My heart was pounding, but across the park, Walcott and Natty sat side by side on top of the picnic table, blessedly

regular and whole and dear in the fresh morning sun.
Walcott's long, long legs folded like jackknives to rest on
the bench. Beside him, Natty's legs were so short that his
feet swung free in their blue Keds. Walcott thumbed at
his phone, probably texting with CeeCee, because Natty
had of course taken over the iPad. Walcott looked up,
smiling, as I hurried to them, but his face changed when
he saw mine.

"What's wrong?"

"We're going," I told him.

But now he was looking past me, over my shoulder.
I turned and saw Hilde Fleming worming on her belly
through the clear plastic tunnel that connected the forts.

"What the what is that?" Walcott said, as she disappeared into the second one. A few seconds later, she
sailed slowly down the slide, her purse across her shoulder, legs together in front of her, primly holding her skirt
down. She landed lightly and stood, brushing at herself.
Then she *waved* at us, all cheery with the bandaged hand,
the one I knew had a hole clean through it. She turned
and trotted off the other way, toward the diner, and disappeared inside it.

"Is that the weird kid from the blood drive?" Walcott
asked, his voice rising. "What the hell just happened?"

"Walcott said *hell*," Natty reported, not looking up
from his game.

I had no idea how to begin to answer. I'd been so re-
lieved in the emergency room when Natty came back to
himself that I'd forgotten her. I'd ignored the whole encounter, assuming we'd never see her again. Big mistake.

Natty didn't need to worry about Hilde, though. He didn't seem to be fretting about the encounter in the playhouse or fixating on the sprig of super-short hair chickening up at the back of his head. I wanted to keep it that way. I pulled Walcott up off the table and walked him a few feet away, out of earshot.

I spoke in a fast, low whisper. "She's not right. She's so not right. At the gym, remember, her mother was telling us that she's some kind of genius? But I think it's going wrong in there. In her head, it's going very wrong. She has a thing about Natty, and I don't think she's safe. She thinks she's magic or something, and she thinks my kid is like her. But he isn't. He's not like her. Natty is just regular."

Natty looked up, though I knew he couldn't have heard me.

"Done!" he said.

He turned the iPad to show us, and I saw he hadn't been playing with Dinosaurs! It was the Rubik's Cube app that had been tormenting Walcott for days. Natty'd had it less than ten minutes, but on the screen, fireworks were going off on the black background, and the cube itself spun in a beam of white light.

I shook my head no, because it wasn't possible. He was three. No way was it possible. And yet he grinned at me so proudly, lofting the iPad where the cube spun, finished and whole, each side a smooth plane of a single color.

Chapter 4

Walcott and me, we did what we should have done the second Hilde Fleming got freaky with a nail at the blood drive: We went and told on her to all our mothers.

Mimmy first. I had Walcott keep Natty occupied with Legos in the den because my kid had a vivid imagination. He was plenty good at inventing his own closet bogeys and under-bed monsters without having to deal with a real one.

Mimmy was fresh out of the shower, getting ready for work. I barged into her bathroom and got her up to speed as she sat in her silky robe at her vanity, moisturizing. She remembered Hilde from the hospital. The idea that the girl had put that nail through her own palm to follow us deeply alarmed her, and by the time I got through the haircut up in the play fort, she looked as concerned as I was.

"I think I should talk to her mother," Mimmy said. "This kid's in trouble."

It took me a sec to realize she meant Hilde. I didn't think of Hilde that way. She was six years younger than me, sure, but she'd graduated high school. She was about to be a college girl, like me. In my mind, Natty was the kid in trouble. Hilde was something awful, looming over him with wicked, silver scissors, out to get a piece. And that rich, low-country mother, bragging about Elon University and early graduation when Hilde was maybe ninety pounds and sickly pale—she struck me as oblivious and smug. "If that woman was any kind of decent mother, don't you think she'd notice Hilde going off the rails?"

Mimmy said, "I certainly would have. I hope. But the girl did make a big point of telling you that no one else could know. Maybe she's tamping it down around her family?"

My head shook in an inadvertent, instant no; I couldn't absolve Mrs. Fleming that easily. Even if Hilde's crafty mind was protecting its own crazy by telling her to keep it secret, even if she wasn't announcing to her mom that she was God's particular, best daughter, I'd known Hilde was off the second I laid eyes on her. I'd seen it, and I didn't even love her.

"Her mother should have noticed *something*. The notebook—No one could see those crazy, inked-up pages and not pause. The nail! Where in a high-school gym is she going to fall on a nail like that? If the mom's this blind, talking to her could make things worse. We have to think about Natty."

Mimmy pursed her lips, thinking. "I tell you what, I'll call around first and find out who these Flemings are and where they're staying. Maybe someone here in town knows the family and can help us figure out the best way to handle them."

I gave her a grateful kiss and said, "Yes. Be sure you find out when their rental ends. That's the main thing."

I left her to dress and went back to the living room. The boys were still in the den, but they weren't playing Legos now. Walcott lounged on our old toile sofa, while Natty sat cross-legged on the floor at his feet. Natty had the iPad.

"What's he doing?" I asked Walcott, and my voice came out sharp.

"I downloaded another puzzle. It's kinda like Rubik's, but it's supposed to be tougher," Walcott said, and instantly my ribs cinched in, squinching half my air out. "I want to see if he—"

I was already zooming across room, moving so fast that Walcott stopped midsentence to watch me with his eyebrows rising. Natty was wholly absorbed, concentrating so hard his tongue poked out between his lips. I wanted to take my finger and manually put it back. On the screen, hundreds of tiny lights blinked in rows, turning off or shifting color as he pressed them.

"Hey!" I said, super perky, and he looked up at me. I put my hands on the iPad. "Mimmy made scones. I bet the ones with chocolate chips. Go ask if you can have one."

I'd smelled them coming in; that was all it took for him to let go and trot off toward Mimmy's room.

"What was that?" Walcott asked me.

I looked at the puzzle. It wasn't anything like solved. My next breath came easier, but I snapped at Walcott anyway. "Don't give him these adult apps."

"Adult?" Walcott said, chuckling. "It's a puzzle, not porn. Don't you want to see if he can do it?"

"Please! He can't do this. You'll frustrate him. He's just a baby, poking at whatever pretty color gets his fancy." No way a three-year-old could solve this thing. Not a regular three-year-old, anyway. Not even a clever one, like Natty. A preschooler who could solve this was stuck way out at the tail end of the bell curve. On the outside of every-thing. A freak.

Unbidden, a memory rose: all the people at the blood drive staring at my son. At first, they'd been so charmed to see a toddler, just turned three, already knowing let-ters. They'd all smiled, enjoying the cute little boy who'd seen enough *Sesame Street* to recognize a big, bright-colored G. But their gaze had changed when Natty said he had to run *Go, Indians*.

I realized my head was shaking itself back and forth. No. I didn't want that for him. I never had. When he was a tiny baby, nursing late in the nighttime, I would whis-per futures into the curve of his pink ear, putting them deep inside his baby brain. *Don't you want to be an ortho-dontist? You could give out such cool toys in the goody basket that all the kids would want to come to you for braces. You'd have a wall full of smile pictures, if you were an orthodontist.* I wanted a regular, sweet life for him: a good education, a nice job, a loving wife, some kids. Natty wouldn't be like me. He'd do it all in the right order. He would be happy and kind and safe and good.

Smart but not too smart. Gifted, sure, but not freakishly so. Real geniuses cut off their own ears and failed at interpersonal relationships and killed themselves.

Walcott didn't get it. "Come on, he solved that Rubik's Cube. That was amazing."

My head kept shaking itself, back and forth. No. "If I gave iPads to a million monkeys, one of them would solve it, too, while another accidentally typed out *Romeo and Juliet* into the Notes app."

Walcott slid off the sofa like a long man-ribbon, twining down onto the floor by me. "Yeah, I know it was probably a fluke, but don't you want to know for sure? Look into my eyes, Shandi." He waggled his brows up and down. "Deep! Deep into my eyes! You are getting sleepy. You are hyp-mo-tized. You want to know for sure."

For once his clowning didn't get me laughing.

"I do know for sure," I told him, but I made myself say it gently because I wasn't going to let Hilde Fleming get to me. She was the one who claimed that Natty was world-savior level special, and she was hardly a credible judge. I *knew* Natty. I'd made him in my body. Mimmy had catalogued his milestones in a baby book, and until now they'd fallen on the cute, bright side of normal. Solving that cube was just a weird blip in the regulation happy babyhood I'd been helping Mimmy unfold for him for three years now.

As for *Go, Indians,* Natty must have overheard one of the volunteers or waiting donors read those words out loud. I'd only had half an eye on him because I'd been filling out the forms, and Natty was such a friendly kid. He might have even asked or——As I stood up to go see what was keeping Natty in the kitchen, the explanation it hit me. *Hilde* could have read it to him. He'd passed by her over and over in all his going back and forth. She was a girl who set things in motion; she'd put a nail clean through her own hand to get to the hospital. She could have seen him yelling the letters and given him the words herself, creating food to fatten her delusions.

I needed to quit worrying about Natty. Hilde was the problem.

I said, "Anyway, he didn't solve the new one, so, there you go," just as Natty came back in, his mouth full and most of an outsize scone clutched in one hand. I scooped him up and dropped a kiss onto his chocolate-smeared cheek. "Come on. Let's go see your momses."

"Okay," Walcott said obligingly, but as he followed us out, he added, "He only had the new puzzle for a minute, though. If that."

I ignored him.

We walked over to the B and B. It was faster to hike the wooded cut-through than to drive; Walcott and I had been running the trail back and forth since we were five years old. We swung Natty in between us, but the path was steep. He wanted to stop and sit down on the big fallen tree when we got to the halfway place, a grassy mini-clearing where Walcott and I always met up. Instead, Walcott swung Natty up onto his back and piggied him the rest of the way.

As we came out of the woods, we saw both of Walcott's momses in their gardening togs, working on the beds in front of the big house with all the guest suites. Aimee straightened up and and waved, and then Darla looked up and waved, too.

I peeled Natty off Walcott and said, "Let's go to the cottage?" while Walcott continued on to the big house to talk to them. I took the iPad, too.

The cottage was behind the main house; his momses lived there. It had a big screened porch off the den, and Darla had put this red plastic table and chairs from when Walcott was little out there for Natty, along with a bunch of old toys.

They never locked their doors—no need up here, and anyway they always had a couple-three big dogs who roamed the property—so once I had dragged out the proper Fisher-Price buildings and Natty was happily rummaging about in the box of Little People and accessories, I went on through the sliding glass doors into the den.

I didn't want my back to Natty, though. I sank down on the big blue sofa that faced out to the porch, watching Natty through the glass. He was setting up the farm. I had a strong urge to keep my eyes on him, every living minute.

It was the first time I'd had a second to myself. I woke up the iPad and went to Google, even though I knew from experience that Google could be a terrible alarmist. Hand Dr. Google the symptoms for ringworm, and he'd likely link you right to leprosy. Still, he was the only doc I had just now.

What I wanted most of all was to talk to Dad. He was a real doctor and the smartest person I knew. If he didn't know what was wrong with Hilde, he would for sure know how to find out. He was out of the country, though, taking my spoiled-ass stepmother on a Nile cruise.

I knew Hilde was hearing voices. I knew she was delusional, believing she and Natty were some kind of yin-and-yang messiah. I had a vague idea what those things meant. I had a one-word guess—but oh, it was a scary word.

Staring at the blinking cursor, I didn't want to put that scary word in. Instead, I put in "hearing voices," hoping to get better options. The top links that came back were for an online poetry journal and a creative writing blog. Under those, I found a link to the UK version of WebMD. I clicked to it, and it helpfully told me, "Hearing voices is a common symptom of severe mental illness." Oh, you don't say.

I started over, typing the word in as fast as I could and still have a hope of spelling it correctly: *schizophrenia*.

I waited for the list of links to load: *Symptoms of Schizophrenia. What is Paranoid Schizophrenia?* And *Schizophrenia: Symptoms Explained.*

As I scanned the page, my gaze caught on words: *delusional, suicide, breakdown, psychotic.* That last one chilled me down into my bones.

I heard Walcott and his momses coming through the

front door. Out on the porch, Natty was so absorbed in his farm pretend he didn't so much as look up as they came into the den.

"How're you doing, kiddo?" Aimee asked me. She was long and tall, with permanently wind-chapped cheeks. Her auburn hair was pulled back in a careless tail.

I shrugged. "Google's freaking me out. I'm trying to get it to tell me what's wrong with this girl."

Aimee said, "Speaking as a parent—my first worry is drugs."

I thought about it, but then I shook my head. Every school had drug kids, even mine, way up in our sleepy mountain town. Pot-'n'-'shroom hippie wannabes, mostly, but we'd also had two guys who'd gotten into meth and dropped out and disappeared. I looked to Walcott, but he shook his head no, too. Last semester at Georgia State, he'd had a genuine sniffy-nosed, twitchy cokehead in his modern lit class. Whatever Hilde's problem was, it wasn't any kind of drugs we'd ever seen.

I said, "She's not a burnout. She got into Elon University at fifteen. Whatever's wrong with her, I think it has to have started pretty recently, don't you? I don't think a person could be that crazy and still organized enough to stay on the honor roll."

"What's Google say?" Darla asked, twisting at her silver bangle bracelets. She was more intense than laid-back Aimee. Walcott called her Worrsy-Wartsy because to this day, she told him to be careful every time he drove, even if he was just running to fetch milk.

They clustered around me to look at the screen, Walcott and Aimee plopping down on either side of me, and Darla leaning over the back of the sofa.

"Are schizophrenics dangerous?" I asked.

"I think they can be," Aimee said, concerned.

"I don't know much about it," Walcott said. He pulled the iPad onto his own knees and touched the second link, *What is Paranoid Schizophrenia?*

But it was Worrsy-Wartsy who shook her head no, even as the page loaded. "It's a disease. A frightening one, and schizophrenics need medication and proper treatment, sure, but it's not hopeless. They can lead pretty normal lives."

Aimee craned her head around to stare at her. Darla had once been a very successful investment broker—so successful they had retired to run this B and B when Walcott was a toddler. She was a numbers head, not any kind of psychologist.

"How do you know that?" Aimee asked.

Darla straightened and flushed, a little guilty, I thought. "I don't know much. Just what I said."

"Oh ye god and little fishes!" Aimee said, chuckling, "You've been watching Dr. Drew or something!"

Aimee, who spent her leisure time hiking, gardening, and reading in the hammock, wouldn't have a TV in the cottage, but they had full cable in the guest rooms. Darla had been known to sneak and watch *Real Housewives* and worse. She flushed even deeper, busted.

"So I sometimes flip on the TV when I turn the suites. Sue me. A couple months ago, some channel had an eighties retro weekend, and they had an old, old Lifetime movie on. I remembered watching it when I was in high school. I loved it. It starred Jo from *Facts of Life*."

Aimee was laughing openly now. "Aw, your first crush!"

"Yes, well," Darla said, compressing her lips. "That's about enough from you. The point is, Jo from Facts of Life was a regular, good teenager, great student, and then suddenly, she went full-blown schizophrenic. It was awful, but as I recall, it ended hopefully. All those movies are based on true stories, and this was made in 1980-something. I'm sure treatment options are even better now."

Walcott had been half listening, surfing link to link and skimming pages. Now he was on the Mayo Clinic website.

"Mom's not wrong; Lifetime for the win," he said. "Look, here—the kind of schizophrenic that has delusions and hallucinations responds the best to medication."

"She's not getting any medication, though," I said. "She's running around unsupervised with scissors." In that moment, how I hated Mrs. Fleming, with her designer glasses and her blown-out, pricey hairdo. How could she not see? "And she's obsessed with Natty."

We all paused and looked out at Natty on the porch. At the Fisher-Price Little People Farm, the cow, the pig, and the horse had been in a terrible three-animal crash. Natty swooped the sheep toward them, making vrooming noises so loud we could hear them through the glass. The vrooms changed to the squeal of failing sheep brakes, and the poor fellow careened into the pile.

"This isn't a real diagnosis," Aimee said. "This is just four worried people and some Google."

I nodded. "But that doesn't mean that we won't . . ." I trailed off. What could we do?

"Keep him close," Darla finished for me, and this time Worrsy-Wartsy had it right. As long as the Flemings were in town, Natty would have eyes on him, loving ones, in sets of four or higher.

Natty and I spent the day at the B and B, not heading back to our house until late in the evening, when I knew Mimmy would be home. As we came in, I didn't smell anything cooking, though. Mimmy was sitting on the sofa, looking pensive.

"We're going out to eat," she announced. "How about Blue Moon Diner?"

"Suits me," I said. "Natty, run go potty." Blue Moon was a twenty-minute drive, and nothing made Natty have to pee like getting all the way buckled into a car seat.

The second the door closed behind him, Mimmy leaned toward me and said, "I talked with Doris and Raylinda." She'd named the two biggest gossips in the county. If Doris didn't know it, then it hadn't happened yet. If Raylinda didn't know it, then it never would. "You want the good news or the bad news, first?" Mimmy spoke quickly and kept her voice quiet. Natty was an incorrigible eavesdropper.

"The good, please. Definitely."

"The Flemings have rented the Jerome house, up on Carver Avenue. The father is a named partner in some old-money law firm." That made sense. The dad had to be making some kind of righteous bank to rent that place. It was close to downtown, with high-end finishes and furniture, a tricked-out chef's kitchen, and a huge deck that overlooked one of the prettiest views in Georgia. Mimmy went on, "He's also a workaholic, according to Raylinda. He was only here for the first weekend. Now it's just the mother and the girl."

"How is that good news?" I asked.

"They only have it four more days," Mimmy said, and that *was* good. "Plus, they aren't from Atlanta. They came over from Charleston." That was even better. When they left, they'd be heading east, away from all my territories. Come fall, Hilde would go north, to spew her varied crazies across Elon University.

Natty came out of the bathroom then, and I said, "Did you wash your hands?" He turned around and went right back in.

I still wasn't ready for the bad news. While the water ran in the bathroom, I told Mimmy what we'd read on Google. By the time I was done, Mimmy had come to a decision.

"I know you don't think it will help, but I have to talk to that girl's mother," she said. "As a parent, I'd want someone to talk to me. We can't be sure what's wrong with Hilde, but we can at least get Mrs. Fleming in the loop, and make sure Hilde stays far away from . . ." she tilted her head at the closed bathroom door just as Natty opened it and came out, his wet hands spread wide in front of him.

"Double washed, with many soaps!" he announced, very proud. "I'm hungry."

"We're going out to eat, just as soon as I make one quick call," Mimmy told him.

"Now?" I said, clutching her arm.

"Absolutely now," Mimmy said, adding quietly to only me, "That girl won't be any less crazy if we wait until after dinner."

I wondered if I should make the call, but Mimmy was much better at getting what she wanted out of people. I let her walk off toward her bedroom, and I stayed with Natty. As far as he was concerned, he was having a perfect day, with everyone he loved clustered about, spending time with him in shifts. I sat on my butt on the floor with him, vrooming cars, while Mimmy took on the grown-up, scary business at the back of the house.

It seemed like the phone call took a long time, though. I thought maybe that was just me, until Natty said, "Except I really am hungry."

"I'll go speed Mimmy up," I said.

I stood, but as I went back through the kitchen to Mimmy's room, I found myself walking soft. When I reached the door, I didn't knock, much less go in. Instead I leaned in close, pressing my ear against the wood and listening.

I could hear bits and pieces of Mimmy's side of the conversation. Enough to catch the tone and know that she was angry. Enough to realize she wasn't talking about Hilde. She was . . . defending me? I could only make out snatches, but then her voice rose even higher and I heard, clear as day "—stop digging for the mote in Shandi's eye when your girl has so many beams of pure crazy sticking out of her face, I could build myself a cabin!"

I gulped. Talking to Mrs. Fleming was a mistake;

I'd said so from the start. And Mimmy should never go to war on phones, where her disarming beauty couldn't give her the advantage. On the phone, Mimmy and Mrs. Fleming fought mom to mom, as equals.

"My daughter's delusion? *My* daughter's?" Mimmy was so outraged she was practically squawking. Apparently Hilde's voices were protecting themselves well—she must have told Mrs. Fleming what she'd overheard me say at the emergency room. Mimmy tried again, saying, loud and firm, "You do not know my child. Shandi is not the mentally ill one, here. It's a coping mechanism, and if you underst—"

I pushed away from the door and walked back down the hall. I didn't want to hear it. Not any of it. Mimmy'd lost control of the conversation. She was on the retreat, and Mrs. Fleming hadn't listened to a word she'd said about Hilde.

I went back to the den and helped Natty pick books and a couple of toys to take to Blue Moon until Mimmy reappeared.

"Let's go!" she said, her smile a little too wide to be quite genuine.

All talk of the Flemings was tabled while we ate. Natty stuffed himself on fried chicken and southern green beans and two whole huge biscuits. Ten minutes into the drive home, he fell into a food coma in his car seat.

Once I was sure he was truly out, not just possuming, I said, "You never told me the bad news. When I got home, you said that you had good news and bad, but you only told me half."

Mimmy kept her eyes on the narrow, winding road leading us home. "I think you and Natty should go down to Atlanta and stay in your father's house. Just until the Flemings' rental is up."

I blinked, surprised. For Mimmy, saying the words "your father" without adding a "be" verb and an insult was unprecedented. "You really think Hilde is that dangerous?"

"I don't know," Mimmy said. "But her mother is dangerously stupid."

"What aren't you telling me?" If she was willingly sending me off to Dad's house, even with him out of the country, it had to be very bad. It wasn't that my parents didn't get along. Technically speaking, you had to have contact with someone in order to not get along. I was close with both of them, but I was an unlikely sunny oasis in the otherwise unbroken, silent tundra that had stretched between them the second I got old enough to drive myself to visitation.

"That girl was at the house today," Mimmy said. "I saw her in our yard about an hour before you came home."

I boggled at her. "Hilde was at our house?"

"I think so. Unless there is some other emaciated, pale, black-haired teenager with a reason to be standing in my pansy bed, peering in my window with her big, old buggy eyes."

The pansy bed was in the backyard, and somehow that felt more invasive than a person looking in from the front. "What did you do?"

"Well, it upset me, Shandi, I won't lie. I ran out there to shoo her off, but by the time I got outside, she was gone. Poof. Unless she's faster than a rabbit, she couldn't have gotten back into the woods. I knew she had to go around the house. I almost lit out after her. But then I thought, what if she went the other way? I was scared I might pick wrong, and she'd double back and slip inside the door."

I shuddered at the thought of that: Hilde hiding out in Natty's big closet, the real-life version of the under-bridge troll he was sure had moved in after we read *Three Billy Goats Gruff*. She could tuck herself under our old sleeping bags or crouch behind the toy bins, and then creep out once until we were all asleep. No wonder Mimmy was ready to send us to Dad's.

Mimmy turned onto the curvy, gravel road that wound its slow way up to home. Beyond our place, it went to the B and B, and then on to some gorgeous hiking trails with waterfall views. We were going maybe twenty miles an hour; it was all hairpins from here.

Mimmy said, "I wish we could—"

Then she interrupted herself with a short bark of scream, and I cried out, too, because as we came around the second sharp curve, a man was standing in the middle of the road. I only had time to catch a glimpse of him: short, fat, round faced, grinning. But I knew him. I recognized him from somewhere. Mimmy slammed her foot down on the brake. Not fast enough. The man disappeared, yanked down under the front of the car even as we jolted to a halt.

"Oh, Jesus, please," Mimmy said, half scream, half prayer.

Natty muttered in the back, disturbed but not awake.

Mimmy was already throwing her door open, leaping out and running forward, but I sat frozen. It had happened so fast. The man and his pale, grinning face. I knew him, and now he was under our front tires.

I craned up to peer into the swath of light created by our headlights, desperate, trying to see if the man was all right, and I didn't realize Hilde Fleming was climbing into the driver's seat beside me until she shut the door. She threw the car into reverse. As she backed away, Mimmy rose up, her mouth opening in another scream. Beside her, the man popped up again, too, his whole body swinging back and forth like a Weeble.

For a moment, I didn't understand. I stared from him to Hilde, her pink tongue stuck out between her lips again as she concentrated. I looked to the man, still swaying back and forth, so crazy. He had no legs. He had a round base and no legs, so he couldn't be a man at all.

Then I knew him. He was Mr. Bang, Walcott's old blow-up boxing toy. He was a heavy-duty plastic punching bag painted like a person. Walcott and I used to beat on him, and he would bob down and roll back up, grinning and obliging, ready to be hit again. I'd seen Mr. Bang earlier today, standing in the corner of the screened-in porch by Walcott's other old toys; now Hilde had stolen him, and set him in the road to stop our car. Dear God, she had been at the B and B today, too, watching us.

Mimmy came running toward us, awkward on her strappy sandals.

Natty muttered in his sleep, as Hilde accelerated forward, careening around Mimmy, the driver's-side tires sliding on the steep shoulder. I thought we would go over. I thought we would tip and fall right down the mountain, me and Natty, but Hilde accelerated and dragged the wheel right and we got around Mimmy and went up.

In the rear window, I could only see the vague shape of Mimmy in the darkness, tottering on her heels in the gravel, trying to run after us.

The car took the next curve, and even that shadow Mimmy disappeared. There was only Hilde, revving the engine, taking me and Natty up the mountain, taking us all up into the black.

Chapter 5

Natty, sacked out in his car seat, was the only thing that kept me from screaming and just screaming and just screaming on and on.

Hilde peeped her big eyes sideways at me and then crooned, "My own! My own miraculous!" and I didn't know if she meant me, or Natty, or whatever this was that she was doing with the car. Her own miraculous *crime*?

"What?" I said, because it was the only word I had.

"We are miraculous, me and him," said Hilde, facing forward and creeping up, up, up, talking faster than the car was going. "Him with me, it will work. This time it will work. You'll see, you'll see." And then she said three words that made all my blood stop running and chill into sludge inside my every vein. She said, "We're gonna fly."

Natty was buckled in, or else I would have snatched him and simply opened the door and rolled out and let her go. But I wouldn't leave my son. I knew what she meant to do. We were going all the way up, to one of the spectacular waterfall views. We were going to drive right over it. She meant for us to Thelma and Louise the whole long way down, spattering ourselves across my very own mountain.

In the faint light from the dashboard she looked over at me and she grinned, wildly delighted, like she expected me to grin back. Like I was her co-conspirator. Grinned! With her good hand and her bandaged one both clenching and unclenching at the Impala's wheel.

"Hilde," I said. "My God, Hilde, you can't drive us—" I stopped. The only possible next words were, *off the mountain*. I was so scared of the very words, I couldn't say them out loud.

"Sure, I can," she said, in an oddly reassuring tone. "I have my learner's permit. As long as you're in the car with me, it's completely legal."

She kept right on driving, and my heart kept right on pounding, but in my head, where it mattered, all my panic stopped. Click. It just turned off. My body was still full of adrenaline from when I thought that Mimmy'd run over a person, but I was calm inside now and I could think for the first time since I'd seen Mr. Bang go down under the car. I thought, *This child has a learner's permit*.

She was crazy, but she was a crazy fifteen-year-old girl. A sick one, with arms as skinny as pipe cleaners. She was six years younger, three inches shorter, thirty-five pounds lighter, and I wasn't going to fly today.

I unbuckled myself, scooted fast across the long seat,

grabbed the keys and turned the Impala's engine off. We guttered to a stop, and I jammed the gear shift up into park before we could start rolling backward.

"Oh, no! Oh, no!" Hilde said, turning to me with the dismayed eyes of a child who finds its goldfish floating very still at the top of the bowl. "What are you doing?"

"I'm declining to be murdered," I told her. I pulled out the keys. The dashboard lights went out, leaving us in moonlight.

"Oh, but no, you don't understand," Hilde said. Her voice was a fervent whisper. "Look! Look, the man in the grocery store, he gave me this!"

She reached up to turn on the ceiling light, then scrabbled in the side pocket of her purse to find a square of paper. She thrust it at me. It was a religious tract, the front cover showing heaping piles of hand-drawn people on fire, their mouths open in screams. They were naked, but the artist had them all writhing strategically so that their genitals didn't show. She flipped it open, and inside, she'd gone to work with her black pen again. Whatever the tract had said initially was wiped away by all her curling, smoky symbols and connected letters. "He gave it to me. Don't you understand?"

I shook my head and said to her, very calm and soothy, "The little market in town? That was just Mr. Beardley. He gives those tracts to everyone, because they started selling beer there."

"No, but you see the message? It's all about me and him," she said, her voice rising as she jerked her thumb at Natty in the backseat. He slept on, out for the night, his little chin sagged against the buckle. "You can stay here, but we have to go up. Please, please, let me take him up. I'll show you what we can do. It's all in here!" She pointed desperately at the tract.

I'd kept her talking long enough. The driver's-side door swung open, making Hilde startle and twitch. Mimmy had caught up to us, and immediately, Hilde slipped the tract out of sight beneath her thigh.

"What on earth?" Mimmy said, taking in the whole scene: Hilde abashed in the driver's seat, Natty sleeping. I held up the jingling keys to show her.

"Good girl," she said. "Oh, you good, smart girl."

"Hello, Mrs. Pierce," Hilde said to Mimmy, so polite. Like we'd all met up here for tea.

"Ms. Madison," Mimmy snapped. She'd long gone back to her maiden name. "Good grief, I've torn my feet up, running in these shoes."

Hilde looked down, hangdog sorry; the stern-voiced-mother presence of Mimmy had instantly diminished her. She looked like any kid caught out after curfew. At the same time, she had that tract hidden beneath her leg, and from where I sat, I could see her peeping up sideways toward my corner of the dashboard. She tilted her head, the way she might to listen if someone on my side of the car was whispering to her. Probably, someone was.

It was so ridiculous that I started laughing, quiet, so as not to not wake my boy, and I couldn't stop. My whole body shook and shook with it.

"Where is your mother?" Mimmy said to Hilde, still very stern.

Hilde shrugged. "She went antiquing. And then to eat. I didn't want to go."

"Where on earth does she think you are?"

"She thought I was at home, earlier. Now she thinks I've gone to that teen movie night they're having at the coffee house. We saw the poster." Hilde said, and added, almost abashed. "I've been texting her so that she wouldn't fret. She's such a fretter."

I gaped at her, trying to get my breath back from the laughing. It was such a normal teenager thing to say. It reminded me of Walcott, right after he got his license, calling Darla Worrsy-Wartsy as he sped us fast over the railroad tracks to make the car go airborne. It was so easy to forget that Hilde, possible daughter of God and definite Flight Risk, was, in her mother's eyes, a regular teenager who could walk herself downtown to have a sugared-up iced coffee drink and watch a PG-13 movie.

Mimmy said, "Scoot your little butt right over, young lady. We're taking you home."

Hilde palmed her tract and then slid to the middle of the Impala's old school bench seat as I shuffled back to my place. We both buckled ourselves in. Her frail knees spiked up as she rested her feet obediently on the hump.

I reached across her to hand Mimmy the keys. She turned off the overhead light and said, "Call Walcott, please, Shandi. I want to drop off Natty with him before we go. We're going to have a good, hard talk with Hilde's mother." She started the car and began driving, forward and up, toward our house and the B and B.

I called Walcott, trying to come up with a super-short, expurgated version as it rang. Hilde hunched down even deeper, sinking to a little miserable bow shape. In the small slice of seat between the two of us, she still clutched her tract out of Mimmy's sight, her thumb petting sorrowfully at the naked burning people as Walcott picked up.

I said, "Hey! We're almost to your place. Hilde tried to carjack me. She isn't good at it. We've kinda reverse carjacked her and now we need to drive her home and have a Come to Jesus with her mother. Can you help me?"

There was a three-second silence and then Walcott said, "That is a lot of information. Whatcha need?"

"When we pull in, can you run out and get Nat? He's crashed and I don't want to drag him along on this particular field trip."

"Absolutely," he said, no pause this time. "I was about to leave for Atlanta to hang with CeeCee, but no big, I'll go tomorrow. Still, this means you owe me the whole story. With harrowing details and dramatic hand gestures."

"Check," I said.

I could hear Darla in the room with him saying, "Harrowing details of what?" I let him go so he could get his momses up to speed.

We pulled into the B and B's circle drive not three minutes later. Walcott did not come out alone. Both his momses were with him, Aimee carrying her socks and shoes and Darla brushing at her hair with her fingers.

Aimee opened the back door and started unbuckling

Natty, saying to us, "We think we should come with you. This woman, she didn't listen to Charlotte on the phone, so why would she listen now? We need to go in there like an army."

Mimmy said, "Thank you, that would be so appreciated," with such immediate sincerity that it surprised me.

Mimmy and Walcott's momses didn't socialize. Oh, they'd always been neighborly toward each other: keeping an eye out for each other's kids, pet sitting, getting each other's mail during vacations. Last year Darla had to have an emergency appendectomy, and Mimmy was the first person to drop a casserole and homemade bread off at their home. But Aimee and Darla's couplehood made Mimmy uncomfortable, and she compensated by being hyper polite. Mimmy was a conservative and a Southern Baptist, which made the momses equally wary and over-mannered. The three of them had never completed a transaction as simple as a borrowed cup of sugar with less than three rounds of please and thank you.

Aimee passed Natty's sleeping body up to Walcott. Natty stirred and his eyes cracked open.

"Hey, Natty Bumppo," Walcott said. Natty nestled into his shoulder, reaching up a sleepy hand to pat at Walcott's cheek.

"My Ucka," he said, using the old, old, baby form of Walcott, and then Nat was back asleep. Walcott carried him off toward the cottage as Darla got into the back on the other side.

We left with Hilde buckled in between me and Mimmy, Aimee and Darla like guards posted in the back,

as if we were transporting a particularly dangerous prisoner. A ninety-pound prisoner with spindly arms. It was
amazing to me how inert and silent and undangerous
she had become, once she had fallen into the hands of all
these mothers.

We drove up to the Jerome house with Hilde barely
present. She didn't speak again at all until we'd parked.
We all got out, and I held the door for her. Hilde scooched
down the seat, and as she climbed out, she fixed me with
her big, lamplit eyes and whispered, "We could have flown.
We could have, if you hadn't been *afraid*." She spat the last
word like it was the worst thing in the world.

I didn't answer. My Lord, what on earth was there
to say?

We walked her to the door in a phalanx, Mimmy on
point, me and Hilde guarded in the center, with Aimee
and Darla bringing up the rear. Mimmy rang the bell.
I don't know what Mrs. Fleming thought, seeing the
crowd on her porch. She crossed her arms defensively,
looking at us all, but the person she addressed was Hilde.

"Sugar? What's going on?"

"Well, she wasn't at the movie, I can tell you that,"
Mimmy said.

Hilde slithered around Mimmy. As Mrs. Fleming
stepped back, widening the door to let her child in, Mimmy
and tall Aimee crowded in, too. We all did, spilling over
the threshold into the Jerome house's vaulted foyer, so
brightly lit, with its butter-cream walls and marble floors.
The Jeromes had entirely avoided the cabin look.

"She was at my house," Mimmy continued, as Hilde

went to the stairs and climbed four of them, then turned and sat down on her butt to watch us. "She was at my house stamping down my pansies to peer into my window. Tonight, she was out stealing my car."

Mrs. Fleming's eyes widened. "Hilde would not steal a car."

"Sure, she would," Aimee said. "Your kid is a mess."

"We would have minded the car theft much less if Charlotte's three-year-old grandson hadn't been asleep inside it at the time," Darla chimed in, her voice harder than I had ever heard it in my whole life.

Mrs. Fleming shot a look at Hilde, but Hilde was no help. She sat on the stairs, fiddling with the zipper of her purse.

"These things you are saying," Mrs. Fleming said, "They are ludicrous. And if you don't get out of here right now, I'm calling the police."

"I wish you would," Aimee said. "I wanted to drive your kid straight to the police myself. Darla is a softer-hearted creature than I am."

It went downhill from there. Mrs. Fleming started asking, very loudly, if we knew who her husband was— never a good sign—and everyone kept threatening back and forth to call the police on everyone else, no one actually doing it because they were too busy arguing about who was crazy and who was lying.

I tuned them all out and looked at Hilde. I could see it now, the child in her. I could see why Mimmy had called her a kid and said she was in trouble. Her skinny arms were looped around her knees as she watched this all play out, her head tilted toward her angels, listening. They were so real to her that I could almost see them, too.

Her mother couldn't or wouldn't. Her mother was afraid; Hilde was right, it was the worst thing in the world to be. Especially if you were a mother. Mothers couldn't afford the luxury of that specific kind of fear. And I was one of them. I was one of these mothers.

I watched these four women tearing into each other, threatening and angry, all of them so mighty because a child they loved was threatened. I'd learned that kind of bravery myself, in the playhouse. But now I thought that it was the easy kind. Every mother had that kind in spades; it was an animal thing, an instinct that rose up whether you wanted it or not.

There was another kind of brave that mothers had to be. This kind was much harder. This kind let you look at your kid and really see them. Not what you wanted them to be. Not all your hopes. Not a chance to fix everything that you'd done wrong, and get everything you'd screwed up done in the right order. Just as a person. Just as the most beloved little person in the world, the one who wouldn't eat peas and who loved fire trucks and who once wept himself sick, he was so sorry he'd burned up an ant with his magnifying glass.

Right as I thought this, there was a pause, a breath of time when every yelling mother had to inhale. Into that second of fraught silence, I said, "I have to take my kid to see a doctor."

It was off beat enough to shut them down for another second, to turn them all to me, and I took a page from Mimmy's book. I stepped into that space, right into the middle of all of them, and then I kept it. Not with pretty. I didn't have my Mimmy's pretty. But I had something else, rising new inside me.

What had Hilde called Natty in the car? *My own,* she'd said. *My own miraculous.*

That was exactly right.

Natty was my own. My own miraculous. No noun, yet. He was my own miraculous *something,* and whatever noun went in that slot, Natty would become it all himself. Becoming exactly Natty, that was his job. My job was to love him, no matter what nouns appeared there as he grew and changed.

Hilde was her mother's own miraculous, and I knew the noun Hilde had in that slot now. Hilde was Mrs. Fleming's own miraculous sick baby, who so badly needed help.

Mrs. Fleming didn't want to see it. Mrs. Fleming was afraid. She was loving the kid she wanted, defending the kid she made up to please herself, blind to the kid who was hearing angels and driving nails clean through her hand. Not from meanness, but because she so badly wanted Hilde to be okay, to fit in and be normal, to be happy and regular and safe. And wasn't that what every mother wanted?

Into the space I'd claimed, I said to all of them, but mostly Mrs. Fleming, "I have a son. You saw him at the blood drive. He's so beautiful. I know you saw Natty do

something in that gym that wasn't normal. He sight-read
a banner, and he's barely three. That's not right. What
you don't know is, Walcott and I saw him solve Rubik's
Cube in under ten minutes. I couldn't solve it if you gave
me ten days. That's not what a three-year-old does. It's
so far out from what a toddler should be doing that I'm
scared for him." Tears welled in Mrs. Fleming's eyes and
her nostrils flared. I kept on talking, keeping the space,
because there were five whole mothers in the room now.
"If Natty's that different, how is school going to work for
him? How will he ever make friends? I'm really scared.
But next week, I'm going to take him down to Atlanta,
and I'm going to have him tested, anyway. Whatever's
going on with him, I need to know. Because if he's going
to be that different, he's going to need help. I have to
help him. Me. Because I am his mother."

There was a pause and we all heard Mrs. Fleming
swallow. Her eyes cut to Hilde, quiet on the steps, and
then away. She brushed at her eyes with her hand, and
then looked at it, surprised, I think, to find her hand so
wet.

Hilde sat, not looking back. Listening, but not to us.

"Natty did what?" Mimmy said.

"Not now," I told her quietly. "It's time for us to go
home."

Darla said, "But she——"

"Darla," I cut her off, speaking firm, mother to mother.
I was her equal now in a way I'd never been before. I think
she heard it in me, too, because she stopped. "Let's go."

So we did. We trooped back out the door in single

file, Darla, then Aimee, then Mimmy, and me last of all. We left them there, Mrs. Fleming crying and crying under the cut-glass chandelier in that beautiful, vaulted foyer.

As I closed the front door soft behind us, Mrs. Fleming was staring at her broken child as if Hilde was something frightening, but also undiscovered. Something that she had never seen before.

Chapter 6

The next morning, I met Walcott at the halfway place to retrieve Natty. My way, it was all uphill, while his way was an easy trot down. When I arrived, Walcott was already lounging on the fallen tree. Natty was running some kind of matchbox-car construction project in the grassy part of the mini meadow.

"Hi, Mommy. Aimee let me eat all the bacon that I wanted," Natty reported.

"Yum. Sounds like it was a bad day to be a pig," I said. I dropped a kiss on his head, then went to sit down by Walcott on the log.

"We still on red alert?" he asked.

I shook my head. "Mrs. Fleming called the Jeromes last night and cancelled the rest of the rental. They lit out this morning, very early, in a white Cadillac. This year's model. Mimmy got all that straight from Raylinda Dobbs, so you know it's gospel."

"Down to the color of the car," Walcott said. "Good deal."

I kicked my shoes off and let my toes squinch into the grass. Mimmy thought they'd just left to get away from *us*, but not me. I knew we wouldn't ever see them again, but I wasn't worried about Hilde. Her mother would find out what she needed, and she would get it for her. It's what I would do, and I'd seen right down into the very bottom of Mrs. Fleming last night. We were more than a little bit alike.

Walcott's iPad was beside him on the log, and I reached over him and got it. I flipped the cover open and found that puzzle app, the new one, with all the switching lights. The one that was supposed to be harder than the Rubik's.

I called, "Hey Natty, you want a turn with Walcott's puzzle?"

"Yes, please!" Natty got up and trotted over immediately. The kid loved him some screen time, and he didn't get a lot. He toted it back to the patch of grass with all his matchbox cars and sat down.

Walcott was looking all askance at me.

"What?" I said.

"Nothing. Just, you ate my head off like a sexed-up praying-mantis lady when I tried to let him play that before."

I smiled and I took his hand.

"We need to know for sure," I said, even though I did know, mostly.

I'd already called my dad to ask for help, interrupting

his vacation and irking my easily irked stepmom. Dad was probably the best heart surgeon in Georgia; he had all kinds of connections. He'd known at once who Natty should see, and he promised he'd get Natty an appointment, immediately.

Watching Natty poke at the screen now, his forehead crumpling up as he concentrated, I had the weirdest déjà vu. I felt exactly as I had that day three years and seven months ago, when Walcott and I sat in my bedroom with a pregnancy-test stick under a Kleenex, waiting to know what miracle would happen. Waiting for a pink plus sign to confirm what I already knew inside my heart.

I was so glad again to have Walcott here with me. I turned his hand in mine, and I ran my finger over the thin ridge of the scar in the middle of his thumb. He got it here at the halfway place, sitting on this very log with me. Twelve years ago.

It was his ninth birthday. Aimee had wanted to give him a big Swiss Army knife with several blades, plus scissors and a corkscrew. She'd grown up on a farm out west with three big brothers; by the time she was nine she could whittle a cardinal that you could blow against to make a birdcall sound. Darla, on the other hand, grew up in the city, the only child of university professors. She'd wanted to raise Walcott with only nonaggressive toys. Not gender-neutral things; it was "boy" stuff, just peaceful: racing cars and dump trucks, Lincoln Logs and Lego sets.

By the time he was four, Walcott was eating his toast into a gun shape and pointing it at the dog, yelling, "Pew!

Pew! Pew!" while Frisco wagged and grinned up at him, hoping he would drop the buttered weapon. Darla caved and let him have water guns, lightsabers, and Mr. Bang. But no BB gun, like many country boys had. No Swiss Army knife. She drew the line at any weapon that was "real."

The mini pocketknife with its one dull blade was a compromise.

Ironically, it was Darla who gave him the idea that we should cut ourselves open with it. They'd been reading *The Adventures of Tom Sawyer* together. That book, the knife—what nine-year-old boy worth his salt wouldn't want to make his best friend into a blood brother?

We knew that even Aimee would object to this idea, so we met up at the halfway place to do the deed. We sat facing each other, straddling our fallen tree, horsey style. He unfolded the blade, which, small and dull as it was, looked plenty wicked to me, shining in the dappled sunlight.

"Gimme your thumb," he said.

I shook my head, "No, thank you."

I hadn't liked the knife idea from the start, even though I very badly wanted to be blood brothers. I'd brought a safety pin from home, and I held it up and showed it to him. He rolled his eyes at me, silently calling me a wuss, or maybe he didn't think the pin would do the job. I popped it open and before I could think, I jabbed my thumb with it, right at the ball. It hurt, but I didn't so much as peep. I pulled the pin out, and we both peered at my thumb, blank and whole.

Walcott said, "It's no good."

I squeezed at my thumb, and a single bead of blood rose up, red and round. Walcott gave me an approving nod.

I offered him the pin, but he shook his head. He put the knife against the ball of his own thumb and sliced lightly down. Nothing happened. The blade was too dull. He tried again, harder. Nothing, and then again, until he was pretty much sawing at himself.

I offered him the pin once more, but by then he was ticked off. He lay his hand down on the tree trunk, palm up.

I had an inkling of what he was going to do. It was a bad idea. Even as my mouth creaked open, way too slow, he was driving the knife straight down, with all his weight behind it. Right into his thumb.

Walcott sucked in air, but it seemed to get stuck in his throat. I leaned over, staring at his terrible hand. The blade was in his thumb, all right. The pointy tip was sharper than the edge. A good third of the blade had buried itself into the real, true meat of him. He made small air-choking noises, and he was so pale even his lips were white. He lifted his stabbed hand up, and the blade stayed in. He turned it palm down and still it stayed in, a thin line of red running down into the workings of the hilt. I could see the tip of the blade pressed against his thumbnail from the inside.

I leapt to my feet.

"I'm going to get Mommy," I said, my fear regressing my mother's name back to its babiest form.

Walcott said, "No! Wait!" I paused, and he held his hand out with the knife hanging down out of it and a few drops of blood falling down to spatter on the log. "Blood brothers! We have to finish."

His blood looked redder than mine. Maybe only because there was so much more of it. I was so proud of him then, of how tough he was. He wasn't even crying much, just a few tears leaking out his side eyes. I came back to him, and I pressed my thumb with its single smeared bead, up against the slick surface. I could feel his heartbeat in it. I could feel the side of the knife, cool against my hot skin.

I held my thumb to his until he nodded, satisfied.

"Good deal," he said, and then I walked him back to the B and B to get yelled at, to get stitches and a tetanus shot, to get a thousand what-did-I-tell-yous from a distraught Darla, and to get the little scar I could still feel to this day. The same scar he pressed against my hand the last time I was this far outside my comfort zone. The day we knew for sure that there would be a Natty.

Now Natty looked up from the iPad. He turned it toward us. All the lights were golden, shining in perfectly solved, uniform rows. He'd done it. I looked down at my watch. Six minutes.

"Holy shit," Walcott breathed out, so soft that I only could hear.

I exhaled, very slow, and nodded. "I'm taking him to see a child psychologist that my dad knows down at Emory next week. He'll give Natty some IQ tests and stuff like that. Tell us where we stand."

Walcott nodded. "This reminds me of the day, you know, when—"

"I know," I interrupted him.

Natty set the iPad aside, like what he'd done was no big deal. He turned back to his matchbox cars, making vrooming noises as he moved them. Like any three-year-old might do. Beside him, the winking lights in perfect rows knew better.

I held tight to Walcott's hand, and I thought to myself, *There are only two things I want Natty to know about that day, the day we found out he was coming.*

Not that I said, *Shit!* Not how scared and sick I was. Not that I had little red tongues of panic and disbelief come licking up all through me, just like now.

Only two things. First, that though Walcott wasn't his father, twenty seconds after we knew he existed, Walcott was all the way on board. And second? I want him to know the image that came into my head when I knew he was a real, true thing, alive and inside of me.

It was presents. Presents and a cake and a single word: *Surprise!*

A wonderful word, shouted loud and bright, coming from the mouths of everybody dear to me.

If you loved *My Own Miraculous*,
don't miss Joshilyn Jackson's
smart, gorgeously written novel,

SOMEONE ELSE'S LOVE STORY

Available in hardcover December 2013
from William Morrow.
Keep reading for a sneak peek . . .

It seems like an ordinary hot summer day. Single mom Shandi Pierce, her three-year-old son, Natty, and her best friend, Walcott, stop for gas at a Circle K. While Walcott fills the tank, Shandi and Natty go inside the store for a cold drink. Shandi is in line, eyeing a very good-looking man, when the door opens and a stumpy guy with a baseball cap pulled low over his forehead walks in. In his hand is a rusty, old silver pistol.

Minutes later there's been a shooting, and everyone in the store is on the floor, taken hostage. All of these strangers are carrying secrets that will cause their lives to intersect in a most surprising way.

Chapter 1

I fell in love with William Ashe at gunpoint, in a Circle K. It was on a Friday afternoon at the tail end of a Georgia summer so ungodly hot the air felt like it had all been boiled red. We were both staring down the barrel of an ancient, creaky .32 that could kill us just as dead as a really nice gun could.

I thought then that I had landed in my own worst dream, not a love story. Love stories start with a kiss or a meet-cute, not with someone getting shot in a gas station minimart. Well, no, two people, because that lady cop took a bullet first.

But there we were, William gone still as a pond rock, me holding a green glass bottle of Coca-Cola and shaking so hard it was like a seizure. Both of us were caught under the black eye of that pistol. And yet, seventeen seconds later, before I so much as knew his name, I'd fallen dizzy-down in love with him.

I've never had an angel on my right shoulder; I was born with a pointy-tailed devil, who crept back and forth across my neck to get his whispers into both my ears. I didn't get a fairy godmother or even a discount-talking cricket-bug to be my conscience. But someone should have told me. That afternoon in the Circle K, I deserved to know, right off, that I had landed bang in the middle of a love story. Especially since it wasn't—it isn't—it could never be my own.

At eleven o'clock that same morning, walking into gunfire and someone else's love story was the last thing on my mind. I was busy dragging a duffel bag full of most of what I owned down the stairs, trying not to cry or, worse, let my happy show. My mother, never one for mixed feelings, had composed herself into the perfect picture of dejection, backlit and framed in the doorway to the kitchen.

I wanted to go, but if I met her eyes, I'd bawl like a toddler anyhow. This tidy brick bungalow on the mountainside had been my home for seventeen years now, ever since I was four and my parents split up. But if I cried, she'd cry, too, and then my sweet kid would lose his ever-loving crap. We'd all stand wailing and hugging it out in the den, and Natty and I would never get on the road. I tightened my mouth and looked over her head instead. That's when I noticed she'd taken down the Praying Hands Jesus who'd been hanging over the sofa for as long as I'd had concrete memory. She'd replaced him with a Good Shepherd version who stopped me dead in the middle of the stairs.

The new Jesus looked exactly like her.

He was super pretty, slim and elegant. He was backlit, too, standing in front of a meadow instead of a kitchen, cradling a lamb instead of a spatula. My mother had never once gone into direct sunlight without a hat and SPF 50, and this Jesus shared her ivory-bloom complexion. I looked more Jewish than he did. They had the same rich brown hair glowing with honey-gold highlights, the same cornflower blue eyes cast sorrowfully upward to watch me struggle a fifty-pound duffel down the stairs. Neither offered to give me a hand.

Mimmy wasn't anywhere near ready to let me go, and the thought of having to fight my way out of here made me want to flop down onto my butt and die on the staircase.

"Please don't make this awful. This is the best thing," I said, but Mimmy only stood there, radiating lovely sorrow. The pretty my mom has, it's an unfair amount. Simply ungodly, and it worked on everyone, even me sometimes.

"Maybe for you," she acknowledged. "But Natty?"

That scored a hit; I was trading Mimmy's mountain full of trees and deer and sunshine for my dad's three-bedroom condo, sleek and modern, bang in the middle of the city. But all I said was, "Oh, Mims."

We'd been having this fight all week. Dad's condo was ten minutes from the Georgia State campus, and from Mimmy's, I drove about four hours round-trip. I had to register my classes around Atlanta's rush hour and make sure they all met either Tuesday/Thursday or

Monday/Wednesday/Friday. This was enough to make a simple coffee date an exercise in logistics, and Mimmy didn't help my social life go easier. She'd been boycotting anything with a Y chromosome for going on seventeen years now. Even her cat was female, and she'd been known to change my shifts at her candy shop if she knew I had a date. I would've moved to the condo long before if my stepmother, Bethany, had ever let my father make the offer.

She hadn't. Not until last week, when the results of Natty's tests came back. Dad had set them up after Natty taught himself to read. The tests said my kid was rocking an IQ north of 140, which put him firmly in the genius category. My three-year-old could probably apply to freakin' Mensa.

Bethany—Bethany herself, not Dad—called to tell me I could have the condo. This was unusual. Bethany was the heavy who told me I was getting uninvited from Passover because her entire family was coming and the dining room table only had so many leaves. A few days later, Dad would do something huge and beautiful and thoughtful for me, as if these events were wholly unconnected. But this time, Bethany had wanted to talk to me badly enough to dial Mimmy's house phone when she missed me on my cell. A risky move. Mimmy and Bethany were matter and antimatter. Contact between them could trigger a blast that would knock the planet clean off its hinges and plummet us all right into the sun.

Luckily, I was the one who picked up. We had the briefest exchange of cool politenesses, and I waited for her to drop whatever awful bomb she'd primed this time. She cleared her throat and delivered what sounded like an overrehearsed monologue:

"So! Given Nathan's unusual intellect, David wants to help you place him at a more academically focused preschool. We understand how limited the choices are out there in the weeds."

I swear I could *hear* the narrow nostrils of Bethany's long, elegant nose flaring in distaste through the phone as she said that last bit. It was a carefully worded piece of code. Last year, I'd almost killed my Jewish father by sending Natty to preschool at Mimmy's Baptist church. Natty and I no longer attended synagogue *or* church, which was better than when I was a kid and had to go to both. Dad offered to pay all tuition if I moved Natty to a "better" school.

"Surely there is more than one close preschool," he'd said.

"Of course," I'd told him. "If you prefer, Natty can go to the one run by the Methodists."

Now Bethany went on, "It means moving to Atlanta. I know that your mother isn't likely to see this as an opportunity. Country people can be shortsighted, especially when it comes to education. But the benefits . . . I think any decent parent could see them." She sniffed a little huff of disparaging air and finally came to the heart of it. "You and Natty could stay at the condo. We'd put your own phone line in, and you could decorate the third-floor bedrooms as you please. I'm not sure your father is prepared to suffer the on-call rooms with the residents, so sometimes you'd have him napping in the master. But otherwise, you could think of it as your own place." There was a pause, and she added, pointedly, "For the year." Then, in case I hadn't gotten it, "Until you graduate, I mean."

This was an amazing number of long-standing, guaranteed fight starters to pack into a single speech. Even a dig at Lumpkin County! Sure, we were rural, but not the kind of rural in *Deliverance*, and she damn well knew it. If she'd hoped to goad me into turning down the condo I'd been coveting—fat chance. I summoned all my inner sugar and said, hell, oh hell, oh hell-hell yes, and then I got off the phone fast as I could.

Now I dumped my heavy duffel by the front door, next to Natty's *Blue's Clues* suitcase and the stacked laundry baskets full of books and socks and toys. I went to Mimmy and looped my arms around her little waist and put my face in her hair. She smelled like vanilla.

"You're the best Mimmy in all the world. I don't know how I would have gotten through Natty's baby years without you. I couldn't have, not and gone to college. But I'm twenty-one. Natty and I have to stand on our own at some point. This is a nice step."

She shook her head. "You and Natty setting up house ought to be exciting. It's a rite of passage. I ought to sew you curtains and throw a housewarming. But I don't know how to celebrate you moving into that awful man's place."

I let the *awful man* part go and only said, "I am not moving to the *house* house."

Bethany and Dad and my three little stepbrothers lived in a huge stucco and stone McMansion out in Sandy Springs. No way I could ever share a roof with Bethany. I called her my Step-Refrigerator to my mother and much worse things to my best friend, Walcott. She'd earned all her names, though to be fair, I'm pretty sure I'd earned whatever she privately called me.

Mimmy started to speak again, but just then we heard Walcott coming down, his long feet slapping the stairs. He had most of my hanging clothes in a fat fold he held against his chest.

"Why do you have so many dresses?" he asked.

"Because I'm a girl," I said.

My mother eyed my things and said, "A better question is, why do you dress like a forty-year-old French divorcée?"

"I like vintage," I said, going to unburden Walcott. It was a huge stack; I found most of my clothes at rummage sales and thrift shops, digging through mounds of acid-washed mom jeans for the one good circle skirt or perfect two-dollar wrap dress.

He waved me off with one hand, arms still clutched tight around my clothes, heading for the front door.

Mimmy said, pinchy-voiced, "You can't load hanging clothes first. They'll get smushed and have to be re-ironed."

Walcott stopped obediently and draped my clothes over the duffel, giving me a Walcott look, wry and mock-martyred. He'd walked over yesterday from his momses' place to help me pack, as his hundred-millionth proof of best-friendhood. Today he'd help load my car and keep Natty entertained on the drive to the condo. The condo was built in a stack of three small floors. The kitchen and living space were at ground, and Dad's master suite took up the whole middle. Natty and I were taking the two rooms that shared a bath at the very top. Walcott, being Walcott, would carry the heaviest things up all those stairs, while we toted in pillows and Target bags full of shoes. I didn't even have to drive him home, just drop him at his girlfriend's place in Inman Park.

He'd been doing crap like this for me since we were both five, the outsiders at a milk-white elementary school in a so-white-it-was-practically-Wonder-Bread county. I was the only half-a-Jew for miles, and Walcott was the sperm-donated product of a pair of lesbians who left Atlanta to grow organic veggies and run a mountain bed-and-breakfast for like-minded ladies. Walcott's momses engaged in all manner of suspicious behaviors, including Zen meditation and hydroponics. Where we lived, those words were as foreign as Rosh Hashanah or Pesach Seder, strange rites that got me extra days off school and sent me to my dad's place in Atlanta, where I no doubt painted the doors with lamb blood and burned up doves.

Me and Walcott, we'd stood back-to-back with our swords up, together surviving the savage playgrounds; yet here was Mimmy, giving him the glare she saved for any poor, male fool who got caught by all her immaculately groomed pretty and tried to ask her out. She knew darn well that Walcott didn't have a sex-crazed man-genda for helping me move, but every now and then, she remembered he technically belonged to the penis-having half of the human race. She'd flick that suspicious, baleful look at him. She'd done it when he was in kindergarten, even. Back then, he'd showed me his penis on a dare, and it had been an innocent pink speck, clearly incapable of plotting.

"This is the last from upstairs. Let's pack the car after we eat," Walcott said.

"As long as we get on the road by two. I don't want to unload in the dark."

"I'll dish up lunch," my mother said, wilting into acceptance. The wilt was a feint. I caught her sloe-eyed side-peek at me as she rolled away against the doorway on her shoulder and disappeared into the kitchen.

"Hoo! You're so screwed," Walcott said, grinning. To an outsider, my mother would seem to be in a state of mild, ladylike displeasure, but mainly at peace with the world and all its denizens. But Walcott and I had grown up together, in and out of each other's houses all day long our whole lives. He could decode the state of the Once and Future Belle from her lipstick colors and the angle of the tortoiseshell combs in her hair almost as well as I could.

"She's loaded for bear. And I'm bear," I said.

"I can't help you with that. No one can." He flopped into a lanky heap of string on the wingback chair. "But I could say you a poem? I've been working on one for you, for this exact occasion."

"No, thank you," I said primly.

"It's really good," Walcott said. He cleared his throat,

putting on a faux beat-poet reading voice, really boomy and pretentious. "Alas! The Jew of Lumpkin County, exiled once more. Like Moses—"

"Poem me no poems, Walcott. I know what you use those things for." Before he got hooked up kinda serious with CeeCee, his signature move was to quote hot lines from John Donne or Shakespeare to mildly drunken girls in the Math Department.

"They work, though," he said. "I used to get a lot of play, for a skinny English major with a big nose."

"Bah! It's a noble nose."

"It's overnoble. It's noble plus plus. Lucky for me, chicks dig iambic pentameter. But this poem? It's not for seduction. It's free verse and quite brilliant. You wander forty days and forty nights in Piedmont Park, following the smoke from a crack pipe by day and a flaming tranny hooker in the night."

"You're a goof," I said, but as always, he'd made me feel better. "Stop it. I have to pacify The Mimmy. Maybe we could crawl to the kitchen with fruit? Throw a virgin into her volcano?"

"Now where are you and I going to find a virgin?" he asked, droll.

I started for the kitchen, then paused under the painting. The new Jesus, with his salon-fresh highlights, had those kind of Uncle Sam eyes that seemed to track after me.

Walcott followed my gaze, craning his head back to look. "Holy crap! Where is Praying Hands Jesus?"

I shrugged. "I know, right?"

"Shandi, that's your mother in a beard."

"Yeah. Super unnerving. I don't expect Jesus to be that . . ."

"Hot," Walcott said, but he was looking toward the kitchen now, where my mom was. I scooped up one of Natty's stuffies from the closest laundry basket and chucked it at him. He caught it, laughing. "Aw, don't throw Yellow Friend!" He tucked this most important blue patchwork rabbit gently back in Natty's things. "I know she's your mom. But come on."

I couldn't blame him. My mother was forty-four, but she looked ten years younger, and she was nowhere near ready to recover from being beautiful. If I'd been born with a lush mouth and crazy-razor cheekbones, instead of round-faced and regulation cute, I'm not sure I'd recover, either.

"Lunch," Mimmy called, and we went through to the kitchen table. Natty was there already, perched in the booster so his nose cleared the surface of the high wooden table. Most of his face was hidden by his *Big Book of Bugs*, but I could tell the move was worrying him. All his Matchbox police and EMS vehicles were lined up in front of his plate, and he had big chunks of three of his bravest costumes on: fireman's yellow slicker, astronaut's white jumpsuit, airplane pilot's hat.

"Goodness, Captain Space Fireman, have you seen my kid?"

Natty said, "I am me."

Walcott said, "Weird. How did a Pilot Space Fireman turn into a Natty Bumppo?"

My tiny literalist lowered the thick volume to give Walcott a grave stare. "These are costumes, Walcott. I was me the whole time."

I took the seat by him and said, "Oh good, because you are my favorite."

Walcott sat down across from me.

"Mimmy made cobbler," Natty told me in his solemn Natty voice.

I nodded, taking it very seriously. "Excellent."

"Mimmy says I must eat peas," Natty said next, same tone, but I could tell he believed this to be an injustice.

"Mimmy is very right," I said.

All our plates were filled and sitting centered on the tatted lace mats. My mother took her place at the head of the table, and we all bowed our heads.

Looking down at my plate while my mother had a cozy premeal chat with Jesus, I realized I'd clocked her mood wrong. She wasn't sad or wrecked. She'd made chicken-fried steak and mashed potatoes and peas and fresh biscuits, then swamped the plate in her velvety-fat gravy.

She only cooked for me like this when she was furious. She thought the meanest thing you could do to a woman was to give her a fudge basket; she lived on green salad and broiled chicken, and Mimmy would have still fit into her wedding dress if she hadn't set it on fire in the middle of the living room when I was Natty's age. Then she packed me up and moved back here, where she'd grown up.

My angry mother prayed a litany of thanks for food

and health and family and put in a word for the Bulldogs approaching fall season. She didn't go off-book, didn't exhort the Lord to bring her wayward daughter to a better understanding of His will. In the past, God's will had so often matched up exactly with my mother's that she found it worth mentioning. But she closed after the football with a sweet "Amen," and I upgraded her from merely furious to livid.

Natty amen-ed and then started zooming one of his cop cars back and forth. Walcott dug in, moaning with pleasure at the first bite. He'd eat everything on his plate and then probably finish mine, and I had no idea where it would go. He was six feet tall and built like a Twizzler.

"Eat up, baby," I told Natty.

"I will. I have to consider the peas," he said, and I grinned at his little-old-man vocabulary.

My mother had served herself a big old portion as well, and she whacked off a huge bite of fried meat and swabbed it through the potatoes, then put the whole thing directly into her mouth. My eyes widened. I think the last time my mother ate a starch was three years back, when Dad paid my tuition at GSU in full.

I always knew he would, but Mimmy worried he'd cut me off once court-ordered child support for me ended. I wasn't eligible for most scholarships, even though I'd been an honor student in high school. I'd spent my senior year at home, baking Natty and studying for the GED. When Dad's check came, she'd gone to the ancient box of Girl Scout Thin Mints in the freezer and had two, which was for her a caloric orgy. She'd purchased those cookies at least four years ago, and she hadn't so much as worked her way into the second sleeve.

Now she sat quiet, chewing what had to be the best bite to enter her mouth this decade, but it was like she wasn't even tasting it. She tried to swallow, then stopped. Her face changed and cracked, like she'd been told she was eating the thigh meat of her dearest friend. She spat the wad into a napkin and stood abruptly, chair scraping against the old hardwood floor.

Natty kept right on zooming his cop car across the tabletop, but I saw his eyes cut after her as she hurried from the room.

"Mimmy is fine," I said to him.

"Mimmy is fine," Natty repeated, zooming his car back and forth to a mournful inner rhythm. "It's only because we are going far away for all eternity."

I was already getting up to go talk to my mother, but I paused. "Natty! We aren't going far, and we can visit anytime we like."

Natty said, "Not far, we can visit," with absolutely no conviction.

"It's going to be fun, living in Atlanta. We'll get to hang with Walcott tons once school starts, and you can go to preschool and make nice friends." I met Walcott's eyes across the table, because he knew *all* my reasons for moving. Up where we lived, everyone knew about Natty's geniushood, probably mere seconds after I did. It had reopened all the worm-can speculation about who Natty's dad might be. Natty, who picked up on so much more than your average three-year-old, was starting to ask questions. Up until this year, his baby understanding of biology had allowed me to tell him the simplest truth: He didn't have one.

How do you explain to a preschooler, even one as bright as Natty, that his mother was a virgin until a solid year *after* he was born? A virgin in every sense, because when I finally did have sex, I learned my hymen had survived the C-section. How could I tell my son that his existence was the only miracle I'd ever believed in?

If neighbors or acquaintances were pushy enough to ask, I told them the dad was "None O'YourBeeswax," that randy Irish fellow who had fathered a host of babies all across the country. But I owed Natty more than that. Maybe a good made-up story? Something about star-crossed true love, probably war, a convenient death. I hadn't made it up yet, mostly because I didn't want to lie to him. And yet the truth was so impossible.

Telling the truth also meant that I'd have to explain how sex worked normally, while Natty was still quite happy with "A daddy gives a sperm and a mommy gives an egg, and bingo-bango-bongo, it makes a baby." He wasn't interested in exactly how the sperm and egg would meet. Much less how they might meet inside a girl before she'd ever once gone past second base.

But Natty had an entirely different question for me. "Is Mimmy going to die?"

"No!" I said. "Where did you get that idea?"

"I heard her tell the phone that she would die, just

die, just die when we are gone," Natty said. I could hear my mother's inflections coming out of him on the *die, just die, just die* parts.

"Mimmy will outlive us all," I said and added sotto voce to Walcott, "If I don't kill her."

Walcott made a smile for Natty and said, "Yup. Mimmy will outlive every single one of us and look hot at our funerals."

"We'll come back and visit Mimmy lots, and she won't die," I said, shooting Walcott a quelling look. "Let me go get her, and she can tell you herself."

I left Natty with Walcott, who, saint that he was, was asking if Natty would like to hear a dramatic recitation of a poem called "Jabberwocky."

I went back to my mother's amber-rose confection of a bedroom. I'd done it as part of my portfolio to get in GSU's competitive interior design program. It was ultra-feminine without being fluffy, and the faint blush of pink in the eggshell walls suited her coloring. She sat in it like a jewel in its proper setting, but just now, she was in a mood much too heavy for the delicate curtains.

"Not cool, Mims," I said. "Not cool at all. You need to rein it in."

I had more to say, but as she turned to me, her mouth crumpled up and fat tears began falling out of her eyes. She lunged at me and hugged me. "I'm so sorry! I'm so sorry!"

I patted at her, thoroughly disarmed, and said, "Momma . . ." My own name for her, now mostly replaced by Natty's.

"That was completely out of line, in front of Nathan. Completely." She spoke in a vehement whisper, tears splashing down. "I'm an awful thing. Just slimy with pure awful, but, oh, Shandi, I can hardly bear it. He'll forget his Mimmy and be all cozied up and close with that man, that man, that dreadful man! Worse, he'll forget who he is!"

I breathed through the dig at Dad and said, "He won't. I won't let him."

We sank down to sit together on the bed, her hands still clutching my arms. She firmed her chin at me bravely.

"I want you to put something in the condo, Shandi," She waved one hand past me. I glanced over my shoulder and saw her favorite picture, from last summer at Myrtle Beach. It showed Mimmy hand in hand with two-year-old Natty, the ocean swirling up around their ankles. She'd blown it up to a nine-by-fourteen, framed it, and hung it in her room. Now it was perched on her bedside table, leaning against the wall. "I want him to remember me. More than that. I want Nathan to never, never forget for a second *who he is*."

"Okay," I said, though I wasn't sure how Dad would feel about me hanging a big-ass picture of his ex-wife rocking a red bikini. I was positive how Bethany would feel. "I can probably do that."

"No. No 'probably.' Say you will," my mother said.

I sighed, but Natty had never spent more than a weekend away from Mimmy. He might need the picture. I could hang it in Natty's room so Dad wouldn't have to look at it. And Bethany never came south of the rich people's mall in Buckhead. If she did drop by for some unfathomable reason, I could stuff it under the bed.

"Fine. I'll hang it."

Mimmy shook her head, fierce. "I need you to swear. Swear by something you hold absolutely holy that you will hang that at the condo, no matter what." Her fingers dug into my arms.

I thought for a second. I'd grown up between religions, at the center of a culture war, each side snipping away at the other's icons until I was numb to much of it. There were not many things I held as holy.

Finally, I said, "I swear on the grave of my good dog Boscoe, and all the parts of Walcott, and—I won't swear anything on Natty proper, but I could maybe swear this on his eyelashes. Those are the holiest things I know."

My mother smiled, instantly glorious, her big eyes shiny from the tears and her nose unswollen. She even cried pretty.

"Good," she said. "Good."

She stood and dusted her hands off and stretched, then walked past me to the bedside table. I pivoted to watch, but she didn't pick up the beach picture. Instead, she reached past it, to a much larger rectangle, wrapped and ready to go in brown butcher paper. It was behind the table, but it was tall enough to have been visible.

"I already wrapped Him up."

I knew what the package was, of course, by size and shape. The Myrtle Beach pic had been a decoy, with the real picture she wanted hung at Dad's place hiding in plain sight behind it. And she wasn't angry at all; I should have known that when she didn't swallow the bite, but I'd missed it. Damn, she was good, and in her arms she cradled Praying Hands Jesus, the Jesus who had hung over my mother's sofa for as long as I could remember. Man, oh man, had I been played.

My mother dashed her last tears away and added, smiling, "I also pulled down this picture of me and Natty. He asked if he could take it."

With that she picked both up and left the room, practically skipping as she went to add the weight of Jesus and herself to the pile of things that I was taking to my father's house.

After lunch, Mimmy had to get to work. She owned the Olde Timey Fudge Shoppe in a nearby mountain village that was surrounded by rent-a-cabins and vacation homes. The village had a picturesque downtown with an independent bookstore, some "antique" marts, local wine-tasting rooms, and half a dozen Southern-themed restaurants. She drifted, mournful, to her car, looking prettier in the sherbet-colored sash-dress uniform than all the little high school and college girls who worked for her. I'd been one of them myself, until last week.

After a hundred hugs from Natty and a thousand promises from me to visit soon, she drove off to hand-dip the chocolates she would never sample. Walcott and I finished loading and got on the road.

Less than two hours' worth of kudzu-soaked rural highway separated us from the city condo, even with the detour to bounce by Bethany's Stately Manor to pick up the keys. Still, it wasn't like The Fridge was going to invite us in for kosher crumpets and a heart-to-heart. I figured I'd be unloaded and moved before sunset. When everything you own will go into a VW Beetle, along with your three-year-old and your best friend hanging his bare feet out the side window, how long can moving take?

We drove along singing, then I told tall tales for a bit. Natty loved Paul Bunyan and Babe the Big Blue Ox, and I had learned the art of packing these tales with filthy double entendres for Walcott. When that got old, Walcott recited poetry, until he got to Emily Dickinson and started freaking Natty right the hell out, what with the corpses hearing the flies buzzing and capital D Death himself pulling up in a carriage. So we canned it, and Walcott plugged his iPod into my port and blasted his Natty playlist, heavy on the They Might Be Giants, as my car ate the miles. We were listening to "Mammal" when I noticed that the kind of quiet that Natty was being had changed.

"You okay, baby?" I called, glancing in the rearview. His skin looked like milk that was just going off.

"Yes," he said. But he added, "My throat feels tickle-y."

I shot Walcott a panicky glance. We both knew "tickle-y throated" was Natty-speak for "thirty seconds from puking." We were in the last few miles of kudzu and wilderness. In another ten minutes, the exits would change from having a single ancient Shell station into fast-food meccas. A few exits after that, we'd be able to find a Starbucks, and then we'd officially be in the wealthy North Atlanta suburbs.

But for now, there was no safe direction I could aim him. Most of his toys were piled high in a laundry basket under his feet, and the thought of cleaning puke out of the crevices of that many Star Wars action figures and Matchbox cars gave me a wave of sympathy nausea. The passenger seat beside him was full of our hanging clothes. Walcott began searching frantically for a bag, and I rolled down every window and hit the gas. A better mother would have realized this move would be spooky for Natty; he got motion sick if he was worried.

An exit appeared, mercifully, magically close, and I yelled, "Hold on, baby!" as we sailed down the ramp. It ended in a two-lane road with a defunct Hardee's with boarded-up windows on one side and a Circle K on the other. I swung into the Hardee's parking lot and stopped. Walcott wedged his top body between the front seats and unbuckled Natty, while I popped my door open and leapt out so I could shove the driver's side seat forward. Natty leaned out and released his lunch, mercifully, onto the blacktop.

"Oh, good job, Natty," Walcott crowed, patting his back while I dug in my purse for some wet wipes. "Bingo! Bull's-eye!"

When Natty stopped heaving, I passed the wipes to Walcott and said, "Everyone out!"

Walcott lifted Natty out and cleaned his face, carrying him across the quiet road to the Circle K lot. I moved the car across, too. Walcott set Natty down and the three of us marched around in the sunshine. After a couple of minutes, Natty's wobblety walk had turned into storm-trooper marching. He started making the *DUN DUN DUN* music of Darth Vader's first entrance, and Walcott and I leaned side by side on the Bug and watched him.

I was thinking we could risk driving on soon when a green Ford Explorer pulled in to get gas. The guy who got out of it caught my attention. Hard not to notice a big, thick-armed guy with a mop of sandy-colored hair, maybe six two, deep-chested as a lion. He was past thirty, his skin very tanned for a guy with that color hair. He was wearing scuffed-up old work boots with weathered blue jeans that were doing all kinds of good things for him. For me, too.

Walcott said, quiet, only to me, "Gawking at the wrinklies again."

I flushed, busted, and looked away. Walcott liked to give me crap because my first real boyfriend after I had Natty had been thirty-five. The guy after that, the one I'd stopped seeing a few months ago, had been thirty-nine.

The guy in the Explorer finished at the pump and went inside. I had to work not to watch him make the walk, and Walcott shook his head, amused. "It's like you have reverse cougar."

"I'm already raising one little boy. I don't need another," I said, arch, just as Natty passed.

Natty said, "I would like a brother, please."

Walcott laughed, and I gave him a fast knuckle punch.

"Maybe later," I told Natty. His skin had lost that curdling sheen, but he still looked peaked. I got my bank card out and said to Walcott, "Can you fill the car up? I'm going to take Mr. Bumppo here in and get him a ginger ale."

Walcott waved the card away. "I got this tank. Grab me a Dr Pepper?"

I tossed him the keys, and Natty and I went on in. The door made a jingling noise as we opened it; someone had wrapped a string of bells around the bar for Christmas, and they were still up.

The hot, older guy from the parking lot was standing dead still with his hands clasped in front of him in the second aisle. He was facing us, towering over the shelves, right at our end. As we came abreast, I saw the aisle was a weird mix of motor oil and diapers and air fresheners all jumbled in together. He was stationed in front of the overpriced detergent, looking at a box of laundry soap like someone had put the secret of the universe there, but they'd written it in hieroglyphics.

Natty paused to scrub his eyes; it was dim inside after marching around in the sunshine. I realized I was staring at the guy, maybe as hard as he was checking out the box, but he didn't even notice. When Natty was with me, I got rendered invisible to college guys, but a kid didn't stop guys his age from looking. Heck, he probably had one or two himself. While I would never be a certified beauty like my mom, I was cute enough in my red and yellow summer dress with its short, swirly skirt that he should've spared a glance.

Especially since it was pretty obvious to me that he was single. Newly. It all added up: the shaggy hair, the interest in detergent boxes. He was trying to learn how to not be married anymore. Divorced guy meets laundry. Walcott said I was getting a little too familiar with the syndrome.

As we passed, I checked his marriage finger for that tattletale ring of paler flesh. Bingo. Add the broad shoulders, the permanent worry lines in his forehead, the wide mouth, serious eyebrows, and there he was: my type, down to the last, yummy detail.

If I'd been alone, I would have sauntered over, done the thing where I tucked my long hair behind my ears, showed him the teeth that Dad had paid several thousand bucks to straighten. If he'd had a good voice, I might have let him take me back to his place and introduced him to the mysteries of fabric softener, maybe let him get to second base on his newly Downy'd sheets. Looking at him, the football player build, I got a flash of what it might feel like to be down under that much man, pinned to fresh-smelling bedding by the great god Thor. It was a sideways thrill of bedazzled feeling, snaking through my belly.

It surprised me, and I found myself smiling. Sex had never quite worked out for me yet. When I looked at this guy, I knew my body still believed it would. Probably. Eventually. After all, I'd only tried sex with two men. Well, two and a half, I guess, because a year after I had Natty, I'd lost my virginity with Walcott, but I didn't count that at all. He'd been doing me a favor, and we'd never even kissed.

Then Natty tugged my hand, steering me past the hot guy, heading for the candy aisle. Since Walcott wasn't there to prang me, I gave myself a half second to check out the ass as I went by. Passed, flying colors. But then I went on, because Natty was with me, which meant no other man in the world could claim more than a look or two. They mostly didn't exist for me in Natty's presence. Not even Norse godlings. Policy.

Natty paused at the treat aisle and said in solemn tones, "They have Sno Balls."

"Interesting," I said, internally shuddering at the thought of Natty puking nuclear-pink coconut down my back as we drove on. "You know what's even more interesting? They have ginger ale." I said *ginger ale* like Mimmy said *Jesus*, walleyed with excitement, using long, ecstatic vowels.

"That's not interesting," Natty said, but he let himself be towed past the Sno Balls with the same good-natured disappointment I'd used to let him tug me past the blond guy.

The refrigerated cases at the back of the store were full of weird zero-calorie water drinks and Gatorade and Frappucinos, all in a tumble. Diet Coke by the Power Milk, orange juices stacked behind the Sprite. While I hunted ginger ale, Natty tugged his hand away to dig his Blue Angels jet plane out of his pocket. He started zooming it around.

I called, "You got ginger ale?" across the store to the scraggly, henna-haired object behind the counter.

"Do what?" she called back. We were closing in on Atlanta, but her Georgia-mountain accent was so thick I knew that she'd been brought up saying *you'uns* instead of *y'all*.

"Ginger ale?" I turned so she could hear me.

"Just two liters. And they ain't cold," she said.

I shook my head and opened the case to get Natty a Sprite, but I didn't have any faith in it. Mimmy had raised me to believe that ginger ale and a topical application of Mary Kay Night Cream could cure anything but cancer.

I grabbed a couple of Dr Peppers, too, for Walcott and me. Natty had zoomed his way over to a tin tub full of ice, and as I passed him on the way to the register, I saw that it was full of green-glass-bottle Coca-Colas. The sign said ninety-nine cents. It used to be only country people remembered that green-glass-bottle Cokes tasted better than any other kind, but the in-town hipsters had gotten all nostalgic for them. They cost two, even three bucks a pop inside the perimeter.

If I'd gotten the damn Dr Pepper, Natty and I would have walked out clean, but I wanted a Coke in a green glass bottle. I grabbed one and said, "Just a sec, Natty Bumppo."

He stayed by the tub, flying the jet low over the ice as I put one soda back. He was in plain sight, so I left him there and headed for the register to pay.

I passed the blond man, still standing at the end of the aisle. He was breathing shallow, eyes slightly unfocused, like he was looking a thousand years into the future instead of at a box of soap.

The girl behind the counter watched me approaching with her mouth hanging slack. She had big boobs, swinging free in a tight knit top that was cut low enough to show me a Tweety Bird tattoo on the right one. Her bobbed flop of dyed magenta hair ended in frizzles, and as I got close, I saw both her front teeth were broken off into jagged stumps.

"That all?" she asked.

"Yes," I said. It was very hard not to look at the teeth. She started ringing me up.

Then the cheery jingle bells on the door rang out. It was an odd Christmas-y sound on a late summer day, unexpected enough to make me look, even though I knew the bells were there.

I glanced at the door, at the stumpy little guy coming in. He had a broad, pale face with a wide nose under a baseball cap, pulled low. Then my gaze stuck. My whole body stopped moving and the very air changed, because the guy brought his hand up as the door swung jangling closed behind him, and I was looking down the barrel of a silver revolver, really old and rusty.

All at once, I couldn't see the guy behind the gun as anything more than a vague person shape. I only saw the shine of fluorescent light along the silver barrel, only heard a voice behind it saying in a redneck twang, "Get on the ground! Get on the ground right now, before I put shoot holes in you."

His voice was low and raspy, like he was talking in a

growl on purpose, but very loud, and I believed him. He would do it.

"On the ground!"

I couldn't move, though. My joints refused to bend and take me to the floor. I was closest to the gunman, by the register, then the big guy in the detergent aisle, and beyond him, standing tiny and alone in the path of the gun as it swept back and forth, was Natty. Natty gone still with his plane clutched in his hand.

I felt my head shake, back and forth. No.

A gun had come, rusted with anger and ill use, loaded and alive in human hands, into the same room where Natty stood in his honorary pilot's cap, hovering his Blue Angels plane over an ice bucket full of Cokes. Natty looked at the gun, his eyes so round that his fringe of thick, ridiculous lashes made them look like field daisies. The gun looked back.

It was not okay. It was not allowed. That gravelled voice told us all again to get on the ground, but I couldn't get on the ground. I couldn't move or breathe in a room where Natty stood far, so far away from me, too far for me to get there faster than a bullet could, under that gun's shining gaze. His little fingers were white, clutched hard onto his plastic jet.

Then the guy by the detergent moved. Just a couple of steps. A step and a half, really. Barely a move at all for a guy that tall and big, but it changed my life a thousand ways.

It wasn't a threatening move. He moved parallel to the gun, and his palms were up and pointed forward in surrender. He sank down, folding into the seated shape that Natty called crisscross applesauce, palms flat on the ground, spine straight.

That sliding half step put his big body between the gun's black, unwinking eyehole and everything that mattered to me on this green earth.

And that was it. That was when it happened. I lowered my body to the ground, and all of me was falling, faster than I could physically move, way further than a glance or an attraction, falling so hard into deep, red, desperate love. I lay flat on the Circle K's dirty, cool floor, but the heart of me kept tumbling down. It fell all the way to the molten center of the earth, blazing into total, perfect feeling for the big blond wall of a man who had put himself between my child and bullets, before our eyes had ever met, before I so much as knew his name.

About the Author

JOSHILYN JACKSON is the *New York Times* bestselling author of six novels, including *gods in Alabama* and *A Grown-Up Kind of Pretty*. Her books have been translated into a dozen languages. A former actor, Jackson is also an award-winning audiobook narrator. She lives in Decatur, Georgia, with her husband and their two children.

Visit her website at *www.JoshilynJackson.com*.

Visit www.AuthorTracker.com for exclusive information on your favorite HarperCollins authors.